I0523491

REVOLT

L. EL

First Edition

Oakland, California

For my brothers

Anthony, Rendell, Garrett and Kawazi:

the ones to whom I owe

my freedom

L. EL's

REVOLT

PUBLISHING
COMPANY

DAAT Publishing Company

Wise Women Health Services Corporation

P.O. Box 25713

Oakland CA 94602

Unattributed quotations are by Lasha Pierce

ISBN 978-0-9888495-1-8

Printed in the United States of America

Contents

1   Arousal *5*

2   Nation Building *15*

3   Damu *42*

4   Foundations *51*

5   The Mark *68*

6   The Call *75*

7   Second Coming *91*

8   Awakenings *99*

9   Sister Love *111*

10   Queen's Horses *127*

11   Blue Strangers *133*

12   Winter Breezes *145*

13   Birth Song *160*

14   Falling Bricks *171*

15   Motivations *180*

16   Home Grown *200*

17   Harvest *210*

18   The Morning After *241*

Chapter 1: The Arousal

Oakland, California, USA

"PUSH, Shanti!"

"I can't. Wiz, it burns! No! No! Pull it out! Please. Wiz! WIZ!"

The young fourteen year-old girl was frantic and out of control. Wiz could see the baby's head peeking out from between her teenage mother's skinny legs and knew it would not be long before the room was pierced with the crackling cry of a new born baby.

Dee paced nervously around the room like a worried den mother concerned about the safety of her young cub. Dee was like this with all of her girls - very maternal and protective. Wiz had asked her on two separate occasions to put her cigarette out when she was around the laboring mother. Dee's eyes were red and wore the fatigued face of a woman who had been awake for days.

"Help her. Wiz!" Dee said. "She can't do it. It's too much!"

"Ashanti!" Wiz shouted in a firm voice. "This baby is going to be born *right now*! You need to focus and let her come out! Breathe her out now, slowly. Dee, bring those blankets from out the kitchen. Okay Shanti, slow, steady pushes…"

It was divine. She was a perfect, six-pound cocoa dream who added a warm glow to the dim room. Ashanti held her in amazement, as the tiny, slippery person cried a soft meow in a kitten's voice.

Dee was fighting back tears and asking Wiz if the baby and Ashanti were all right. All was good, assured Wiz, as she helped Shanti clean and wrap the baby. Before long, Dee was completely taken with and speaking gibberish to the now fifteen-minute-old woman-child. "Divine" was the name that rolled off of Ashanti's tongue as she gazed at the tiny human. And so it was, that the child was named Divine.

Years ago, Wisdom and her husband Masai had converted their basement into a studio apartment with the intent of renting it out some day. It was well insulated, with a thin layer of cheap carpet, now worn and encoded with the path stories of all who traveled across it. As time passed, the studio apartment had evolved into a one room community clinic. Being a medical doctor, Wisdom was sometimes called upon to help with small medical needs of the local people. At first it was home to a first aid station for energetic children in the neighborhood, prone to accidents. Later it graduated to trauma room, community pharmacy, contraception clinic and delivery room.

The wall opposite the door flaunted an explosive mural of Harriet Tubman, her eyes red with fury and the rest of her face a swirl of bright oranges and deep browns. The room's single window would direct a beam of sunlight over her face every morning, as did the moon at night. The other walls were painted beige, and over the years had been autographed by various visitors. Stories were narrated through these walls, confessions made, as well as revelations. Salvation was found in them. The colors of Harriet's face on the wall seemed to whirl and dance as she acknowledged the new life and welcomed her to the Promised Land- the place where all was plenty and freedom could be seen just over the horizon.

Wisdom and Dee first met at a Kwanzaa party several years earlier at the local community center. Those gatherings proved over the years to lend unity to the neighborhood and a sense of oneness. No matter your religious preferences or economic status, Kwanzaa was a time for everyone to celebrate culture and tradition, and for black folks to recognize their commonness.

Deanna, or Dee was a well-known madam in the community. A mid-thirties, caramel tower, with long legs and hair to match, she was at least six feet tall with overflowing breasts, ass and attitude. She ran a very tight and orderly organization with her girls, and she was a smart and practical businesswoman. In her youth, she had fallen victim to drugs and pimps, but she hadn't hooked in over ten years. Now she made her money managing the sexual careers of younger women. She took in mostly teen runaways or veterans of the business who were tired of being abused by male pimps. As far as Dee was concerned, women were capable of making their own decisions about their sexuality and respective worth.

What Dee offered her girls was more than shelter, protection and friendship. She employed a lawyer and three bodyguards, all enforcers of her clients' freedom and safety. She took a small fee of course. But many in the community respected Dee for what she did. They saw her as accomplished- as someone who overcame the obstacles of her youth.

Wisdom, however, could only see her as a stain on society. She had heard of Dee's various escapades, and instantly judged her character as sub-standard. In turn, Dee thought of Wisdom as pretentious and naive, incapable of surviving outside of her limited, middle class environment.

They were pleasant to each other at their first encounter. Each had heard of the other and were equally reserved in the initial interaction. After a little Zinfandel and a lot of Al Greene, they had eventually exchanged a smile or two, and later shared a few moves on the dance floor to the heavy lyrics of Ice Cube. Dee had a sharp wit, quick step and even quicker smile. As the night went on, Wiz found it harder to resist Dee's charm, despite her career choice.

Wiz wasn't the first person Dee had this effect on. Everybody loved her immensely it seemed. But neither Wiz nor Dee would have predicted they would be together in this dark basement coaching Ashanti into motherhood.

Before the baby was born, Ashanti had decided to give the baby up and spend her life as a lawyer fighting to save abused children. She was a runaway, and had been taken in by Dee early in her pregnancy. Dee would not allow her to hook while she was pregnant, so she attended school while awaiting the delivery. She was a great student and well liked at Bay Prep Academy, the local private high school Dee had managed to get her enrolled in on scholarship. She kept a 3.9 grade point average, was elected student body Vice President and loved her role as director of the Big Brothers and Sisters tutorial program. The ability to juggle those responsibilities, despite her home situation, convinced Ashanti that she would be able to continue with school throughout her entire pregnancy. But, in her eighth month of pregnancy, when her oversized clothes could no longer hide her swollen belly, school administrators asked her to leave. Apparently, she was considered a "poor example" to the other students.

Ashanti hated being limited and stereotyped. She hated being punished for her social circumstances.

"I *hate* these fucking contractions!" she said, trying to stifle a yell during the bus ride home from school about a month later. Her water had broken, and Dee was beside herself with worry when Ashanti arrived in a puddle of water and in obvious labor.

Wisdom instructed them to come straight over when she received the call From Dee. After what seemed like endless hours of pain, sweating, panting and screaming they all now stared in amazement as Divine sucked her fingers and rolled her big brown eyes around the dim room to take in her new world.

Ashanti stayed and talked to Divine for a short while before Dee took her home to recover. Wisdom had already made arrangements for the baby to be placed at Mama Pearl's – a house for orphaned children in the neighborhood. Mama Pearl took in mostly babies of drug addicted mothers, abused women, and sometimes teen moms. The agreement was that Mama Peal would receive the infant in October, when she returned from her visit to New York to attend her father's funeral. But Divine arrived three weeks early, and now Wisdom would need to care for her until Mama

Pearl returned. How would Masai and the children react?

Wiz sat in the basement with the newborn all afternoon conjuring up an explanation to give to her husband. She looked to the faded portrait of Harriet, but there was only was silence. Wiz had until six that evening, until her husband would arrive home from picking the children up from after school care. It was now four o'clock and she was running out of time.

Wiz wrapped Divine up and together they went upstairs to the living room. Wiz started a fire, played some music and started dinner. She fed the infant the expressed breast milk that Ashanti had left through a medicine dropper, and planned to go to the market for formula after Masai came home.

When Masai entered, he floated in on the tunes of Miles Davis, the fire glowing on his skin, and the smell of yams, cornbread and baby's breath in his nostrils. He noticed the look of guilt on Wiz's face and braced himself for the coming bomb.

"Hi Mama." the kids all shouted in turn.

"Hi guys." Wisdom squeezed each with the same intensity as when they parted for school earlier that morning.

"You guys wash your hands and get ready for dinner."

"Hey sweets." She kissed Masai soft and slow on the mouth.

"How'd you get here so soon? Got off work early today?" Masai replied, still weary of her overly jubilant greeting.

"I had to leave the clinic this morning after Dee paged me. Ashanti delivered today, you know."

"Oh really? How'd it go?"

"Pretty good. The baby is just a doll!"

"Did she end up keeping the baby or is it still going to Mama Pearl's?"

"She'll go to Pearl's-eventually." her tone now giving clues to the impending news.

"What do you mean 'eventually'?"

"Well for the time being, she's here with us." Wiz braced herself for the coming eruption.

"She's what? Who? Ashanti?"

"No, Divine, the baby. She needs a place to be until Mama Pearl gets back in town. You know she had that funeral to go to."

Wisdom stood staring up at her tall, thin husband with her glass marble eyes begging for his approval.

He knew it was a set up from the start and it would now be impossible to talk her out of it.

"Wisdom," he whined in that *why us* tone.

"Please, baby. Just two weeks."

"TWO WEEKS! Wisdom…"

"It'll go by faster than you think, and the kids will adore her. Think of it as a temporary babysitting opportunity. Come see. She's right upstairs sleeping."

Masai was defeated. Although the final decisions regarding the family were his to make, he rarely told Wisdom no. Her smile and generosity were infectious and he hated to disappoint her.

Iyana, Fumari, and Kikumbe held their breath in suspense as their mother sat and showed the tiny person to them. It was their first time seeing her. When the baby had arrived earlier in the day, they were all at school, and then soccer practice after that. They each took turns holding and feeding her. Iyana especially, was engrossed in the helplessness of this perfectly serene soul. She helped her mother with the newborn constantly, and she openly wished for a baby sister of her own.

Masai remained distant from the child the entire two weeks, and warned Wisdom not to fall too deeply for her as well.

Finally, the morning came when Mama Pearl called to announce her return and inquire about the precious woman child. The entire family sat in mournful silence as Masai confirmed arrangements for the baby to be picked up that evening. They later decided that Divine's departure should be a happy one, and the family spent the day picnicking at a local park. The transfer was arranged after the children were asleep, and Masai new that Wisdom was hoping that he would suddenly change his mind and invite Divine into the family forever. He did not, and he was sure she would survive the disappointment.

Chapter 2: Nation Building

Oakland, California

Wisdom Masters. She had been named by her parents as a tribute to her grandmother "Wise" – the one who first saw her budding potential as a healer at the young age of five. She had always been very driven and determined – some say outspoken and sassy. She was often in trouble one way or another for saying the wrong things at the wrong times. Children were not to vocalize their opinions too often back then – not honestly anyway.

She was the only girl of five children, and her four brothers made sure she was isolated from everyday goings on of the neighborhood. The eldest brother Abu was strictly by the book, and was the conscience of the younger three, Rakim "Sarg", Dubane and Modo. The younger two were close in age and never far from the others' side. Sarg was the strategist of the trio, Dubane and Modo the enforcers.

Wiz was a good student throughout her school-aged career. She had modest looks, at best, but was a dedicated athlete and fierce political activist. She quickly won the respect of most of her classmates in high school, and spent the last three years of high school as president of the Black Student Union on campus. Spinning in a tornado of politics and economics, she was always spearheading some demonstration or another on her high school campus.

"Today's assembly in honor of Black History Month – or should I say *World* History Month, because really, the history of the WORLD begins in Africa…"

Complete silence floated from the audience of young adults.

"All of the major continents were first inhabited by *us*! We authored every major world religion! *We* brought light to the planet in the form or mathematics, science, literature and music! Yes, *we* formed the first dynasty of China, populated Australia and India, brought civilization to Europe and America!"

"Today is to honor our past, present, and future. To acknowledge our ancestors and ourselves. But today is also to remember and mourn those who suffered at the hands of insane European captors. Those who died during the Middle Passage, those raped and abused in Africa, Australia, India, Asia, and the Americas. Those yet to be born and those who have moved on. Today's assembly is to recognize our past and potential future impact on the world as we know it!"

Most of the time, those pearls were wasted on those students too distracted with their own lives to care, but Wisdom was convinced that not all high school students were ambivalent about the plight of Black people and that despite appearances, some people were actually listening.

Washington D.C.

Wiz hit college with the energy of a napalm bomb. She was eager to meet new friends and learn new concepts. She was receiving a full athletic scholarship for basketball and she couldn't wait to compete in college. Two months into her long awaited college career, Wiz hit a wall. She became extremely tired and spent most mornings hugging the toilet with watered mouth and churning stomach. She thought she should've shaken this virus weeks ago, but now after five weeks of misery, she went to the Student Health Center on campus. The nurse took a urine sample and asked her questions about her health.

"When was the first day of your last period?" The nurse was very matter-of-fact in her questioning. Wisdom could vaguely remember.

"I think a few months ago. It's not very regular lately."

"Are you taking any form of contraception?"

"No. I don't need anything right now."

"Ok, well I need to test your urine and I'll return shortly."

A few minutes later, the nurse returned with the news that Wisdom Masters was pregnant. Pregnant? Pregnant! That was impossible! Her episode with Shug had been the first and only time she had ever had sex!

It had been over a month ago. Shug was a childhood friend whom Wiz had long had a crush on since hitting puberty. He was physically attractive, and despite his arrogant attitude and illegal neighborhood dealings, she had felt some peer pressure to engage in sex before college. It was illogical and she knew it. It was even irresponsible since she had stopped her birth control before the basketball playoffs to loose a few pounds only two weeks prior.

Sex with Shug was awkward and uncomfortable. His kisses were overly hard and sloppy wet. He urgently tried to fit his ugly, swollen organ into her delicate middle and she held her breath until the whole horrible thing was over.

Now here she was in disbelief. She stumbled out of the clinic in a daze, searching her mind for the solution to her problem. Yes, this was a *huge* problem.

On the long bus ride home, she came to the conclusion that she would not continue the pregnancy and risk losing her scholarship. How devastated and disappointed her parents would be if that happened. She knew Shug didn't want any more children – he was busy enough shuffling the relationships he already had. Wiz wanted children, but not right then.

She called him up and said she needed to see him, and could he please fly to visit her in Washington D.C. He was on the next plane leaving Oakland.

"I'm pregnant." she blurted out after their initial embrace at the airport.

Shug was at once happy and upset, but didn't show it. He hadn't told Wiz, but he was now expecting two babies back home, each girl due to deliver one month apart from the other. This was the worst time for him to hear those words *again*. But this was Wisdom. He had always admired her and wanted her for his own. And if he was ever going to be a father at all, he'd wanted it to be with her. He said nothing, which she took as a sign of disapproval, and she quickly followed with,

"But I'm not keeping it. Look, I know this is bad timing, Shug and I'm sorry I asked you to come all this way. But I'm scared to get an abortion by myself."

Her eyes were filling with water and Shug's heart weighed heavy in his chest. He hugged her close, a lump forming in his throat the size of a grapefruit.

"Okay, Wiz. It's all right. I'll stay here as long as you need me to."

He wanted to tell her to keep the baby and he'd move out to be with her and help her. But he knew it would only hold her back. He never wanted to see her be held back. He held her hand for the entire procedure and stayed with her for an entire week after the abortion.

They slept in separate places, with Wiz in her bed and Shug on the couch. That was how Wiz wanted it, and Shug agreed. They watched old movies and ate home fries all day, and laughed, joked, and told childhood stories all night. The ride in the cab to the airport was quiet. When they arrived to the curb, Shug opened the door on his side while the cab driver went to the trunk to get Shug's bags.

"You should just come back with me Wisdom," Shug turned to face her in the car.

"No, I need to finish school." Wisdom was clear. "I'll be okay." she said with a confident smile.

"There are schools in California. Plus, your family is there."

"Look Shug." Wisdom was explaining, "I'm good. I am where I want to be right now. I'll come back to Cali when I'm done."

"Well, you can't say I didn't try." Shug closed the door and waved to Wisdom as the cab pulled off. She rolled the window down,

"Have a safe trip!"

The image of Shug got smaller and smaller in the back window of the cab.

College was a new scene for Wisdom. It was the late 1980's and Black folk came in all shades, sizes, and flavors. Special interest groups constantly pushed and pulled the campus administration in often-wasteful attempts at effecting change. Different ethnic, religious and sports groups, the Gay/Lesbian contingent, Fraternities/Sororities, animal rights groups, environmental conservationists and various rainbow coalitions of multi-ethnic origin. The Zionist controlled all financial and governance matters, although they successfully camouflaged this fact with allegations of anti-Semitism at every opportunity. Among her people, rigid lines were being etched in the solid foundation of social and economic divides. The aspiring capitalists in the Black community focused on the right to acquire material assets and be free to oppress and exploit lesser peoples, as European had done throughout history. African Nationalists were separatists, pushing for the emergence of an independent African Nation within the U.S. From militants to spiritualists, ex-cons to silver spooners, African (Black) students on campus were fragmented and self-neglected.

Despite this seemingly tragic flaw, the attraction for Wiz was that they were all thinking, motivated individuals, who armed with a little unity and direction, could become one monstrous, thinking, motivated body, capable of astounding accomplishments. It was all so exciting!

She was suddenly no longer the lone activist she was accustomed to being in high school. She was now a naive, wandering, and eager college freshman in a sea of budding national and international leaders.

Solosi was one of the first people Wiz met on campus and she quickly became entranced. Solosi had always been quite the dynamic speaker, which was why the African Liberation Movement (ALM) always pushed him in front as the spokesperson of the African revolution on campus. Rallies like these were commonplace – usually in response to some recent political atrocity or special anniversary of historic significance. Malcolm X's birthday, proposition XYZ, police brutality, African Liberation Day – all could quickly insight a crowd of political activists to aggregate and ultimately denounce Capitalism and colonialism. The political arena was definitely an electric one, an intellectual battlefield, and passions tended to spiral to limitless heights.

"The challenge we now face as a people is to identify with each other as one entity. When we begin to believe that each and every assault on African people is a personal on against our own person, we will react with a more forceful, effective manner. The police will no longer be able to harass and abuse the brother on the corner. All the African political prisoners in the prison system would be free. Africa would cease to feel bombs on her shores, no World Bank breathing down her neck. Unity brings Freedom brothas and sistahs, so let us enter the New Year in a spirit of oneness and victory!"

The crowd ignited into a blaze of cheers and applause. Wiz soon became intrigued and energized by the ALM. As with most campus-based movements, the focus was political education. Wiz was attracted to the limited potential for violence. ALM was a safe arena for the exchange of knowledge and ideas.

"Our cause is dedicated to the education, upliftment and liberation of African people throughout the world, including those trapped behind enemy lines in the United Snakes of America. We are Black folk born on the continent of Africa, in the U.S., Europe, the Caribbean and elsewhere, a true Pan African representation." Solosi was always looking for new recruits.

The orientation for ALM was held in the student center conference room. Wisdom arrived early and was introduced to several senior members before the meeting began. When the meeting starting, each person in attendance had to recite their name and what they hoped to gain from joining. Lawana, the ALM secretary, opened the meeting with her signature greeting.

"Welcome Africans!"

The debate that followed was the most interesting Wisdom had encountered thus far. What constituted being an African? Being born on the African continent? What about White South Africans? Was it having African ancestry? Couldn't all peoples on the Earth claim such ancestry, however distant? Was is skin color or hair texture? What of Australian aborigines?

"What difference does it make if we strive toward unity with other African people? I am an American. I don't see the relevance."

The woman seemed to speak for many in the room, given the symphony of "Amens" and collective nods of agreement.

"That's right Sis. I am American also. I'll try to give an example. Let's just take Jews in this country. European Jews, not the original Ethiopian Jews, that's a different discussion altogether." The last statement was followed by soft chuckles.

"Because white Jews have unity with the European colony currently occupying Palestine, which they conveniently call 'Israel', they have a more powerful voice within this society. They have a strong lobby and the ability to influence domestic and foreign policy. The same is true for Chinese Americans. Imagine how loud our voices will be when we politically and economically align ourselves with our African brethren and sistren." The applause thundered throughout the lecture hall, the words echoing in Wisdom's head.

Wisdom later became great friends with Lawana and valued the knowledge and experiences they shared over the years. She also met Masai in the same campus organization.

Masai was born in Kenya and was in the U.S. on an education visa. He lived with his cousins, who had been in the U.S. for a longtime and had settled in Oakland. Although not as vocal and aggressive as the other men in the ALM, he was a faithful member and volunteered to teach free Swahili classes to anyone interested. This was were he first met Wisdom. He was studying mechanical engineering, which required him to study for long periods of time, and he was working full-time to pay his tuition.

Despite his busy schedule, he managed to teach the members of the ALM on a biweekly basis, equipped with homework and periodic quizzes. Wiz and Lawana took it a step further and enthusiastically requested that Masai only speak to them in Swahili so they could master the language more quickly.

One day, in the middle of a Swahili lesson with Masai, Wiz would stop and say in English,

"How do you say 'maybe' in Swahili, Masai?"

"There is no such word where I'm from. Africans either say 'yes' or 'no' and mean it. Words like 'maybe' and 'almost' are only a part of the Euro-languages. It speaks to the European man's insecurities and inability to control his surroundings."

Wiz and Lawana looked at each other and in complete harmony chanted,

"Oh. Deep."

Wiz liked Masai's analyses on most things. She liked his ever-thinking, calculating mind and she was at once attracted to the thin, dark, tall Kenyan with deep black marble eyes, curly eyelashes and lips so perfect, they looked painted on. Plus, unlike most in the group, he was humble and quiet: never boastful, arrogant or competitive.

The lessons between Masai and Wisdom became more and more private. She spent time with him even on weekends, at his family's home, all of them delighted and impressed with her quick grasp of the language. They marveled at her way with children, her sense of humor and enormous smile. She was full of life and perfect for Masai as far as they all were concerned. It also helped that marrying an American would almost guarantee Masai's citizenship.

One night, just before taking Wiz home after a family barbeque (she had passed on the goat they had caught and grilled earlier that day, but had her fill of veggies and carrot cake), Masai invited her to go with him for a walk in the neighborhood. On the way back to the house, he stopped her and kissed her slowly. Wiz was pleasantly surprised and shyly kissed him back.

"I'm glad you came." Masai said to Wiz tenderly.

"I'm glad you asked me."

"Wisdom, be my wife. I want you to be my wife."

She was stunned. Not only was that their first kiss, but they had barely even hugged. They hadn't had sex yet. Where was this coming from? Sure, she had felt an intense attraction toward him, and had always known that he felt similarly. But marriage? It was all happening out of sequence, and she hated being unprepared for anything.

"Masai, that's biting off a lot, don't you think? We've never lived together or learned each other's habits. We've never even been intimate before."

"I know, and that is how it *should* be."

OH – MY – GOD! He is on some traditional African virginal trip, Wiz thought to herself. Should she confess that she had been with men before? There would be no tight, virgin pussy to blow his mind on their wedding night, that was for sure. No blood on the sheets to prove to the other men of his wife's purity. She had been with Shug, but that was certainly none of Masai's business. She began to frown unknowingly, and opened her mouth to explain how she was not ready for marriage, when he kissed her again, slower and more deeply than the first one.

"I love you. Wisdom it makes no difference what habits you have or what your sexual practices are. Nothing else matters. I'm sure whatever shortcomings I have, you'll pound them out of me in less than a week." He laughed to himself, and his smile lit up the entire block of darkness.

Before she could close her mouth, before she could contain her heart, before she could swallow her stomach that had made it's way to her throat or fan that burning flame skipping up her back and around her neck to her cheeks – Wisdom said

"Yes."

It was only her second year of college. When they returned from their walk, the family, as if having heard the news from the restless wind, was singing a traditional wedding song in Swahili laced with heart felt congratulations for her and her husband to be. Wisdom was overcome, and beamed in the light of her new family.

By the end of the spring semester, they were married. The ceremony was at the beach at Wisdom's request. The beaches of Half Moon Bay in California can be a bit frigid and windy, but both families swarmed to the ocean-side affair in full force to witness the event, which hosted a full array of bright fabrics, silks, and head wraps. The rhythm of the women's enormous hips swaying in procession folded in with the calm whisper of the ocean wind. Drums screamed out to the ancestors to join the celebration, and Wisdom was called back home to the place of her people's birth. She felt reborn and re-discovered, as if she for the first time realized her ancestry as being truly African. Her parents were still skeptical about the rush of it all, but thought their new son-in-law a respectful and polite enough young man.

By the end of the winter, the couple announced that they were expecting their first child. They had planned to have children early on, so that they could complete their family while they were both young. Wisdom was more alive than ever. She still helped to coordinate the ALM and orient new prospective members. She was studying psychology and actively applying to medical schools in California to be closer to her and Masai's families. She was determined to complete her training as a doctor.

She and Masai had a few science classes together, required of both of their majors: Physics, Calculus, and Statistics. They studied together, attended political meetings together and all of Wiz's prenatal appointments together. Masai worked at night, but not before doing most of the cooking for Wiz. He'd go to school from work in the morning and be done with classes by early afternoon. He'd study with Wiz, tend to any political or personal obligations, and go home to be asleep by early evening. He had to wake again late night, eat, shower, and be back to work by midnight.

The schedule was draining for their young relationship, but each sacrificed without open complaint. They were both in their early twenties and had been married only one year. They spent the entire weekend together however, and after a week of sleeping alone, Wisdom would long for the heat of Masai's long, slender body beside hers. She would make loving gestures to him all week – with notes on the refrigerator, calls to his job, back rubs at the library – leading up to these two short days when she had him all to herself.

Wiz's sexual appetite was heightened with the pregnancy and Masai was always very careful with his handling of her. He loved the way she fit perfectly around him, and there was something sexy about her round belly and full breasts. He would kiss them softly and whisper to her and the baby with every caress.

Iyana was born in late spring, just in time for final exams. Wisdom and Masai took turns caring for their newborn daughter, while the other studied. They were exhausted. They were frustrated. They were unprepared for what marriage and parenthood demanded.

"Masai, could you please get the baby? I hear her starting to stir a bit." Wiz was at the kitchen table with books and papers spread out in front of her.

Masai was across from her with a similar pile of study materials.

"I can't Wisdom, I really need to finish this." He never looked up from his reading.

"That's what you said last time. I need to study too you know." She was glaring at him, clearly upset.

He could hear the anger rising in her voice, despite her obvious attempts to hide it. He met her gaze, bracing himself for the coming conflict.

"Not really. I don't know why you insist on making things so complicated. The baby is here now and you should postpone your studies anyway. We can't go on like this."

"On like what? I have no plans to postpone anything! Why would you even suggest such a thing?"

"Wisdom. Love. We have a new baby. The house is a mess. There is never any food here. With us both studying full time and me working full time, there is never time for shopping at the market, cleaning, or spending time together. That's all I'm saying." He was trying to be as calm as possible.

"So I guess those things are only for me to do?" Wisdom was shouting. "Stop studying and give up pursuing my career? That way I'll have more time to cook and clean? Is that it?"

The debate was a never ending one in their fragile relationship. There was no end, no resolution, no compromise. Masai tired of his wife's stubbornness. Wisdom resented her husband's assumption that her aspirations were expendable or worthy of delay. And to make things worse, his mother was a constant, nagging reminder of just how different gender roles were thought of in his native country.

"You spoil her. That is the source of your problems." Mama Masai told him over the phone. She scolded him often regarding his apparent inability to control his American wife.

In their village, a mother was called by the name of her first born. Thus, Wisdom would be called Mama Iyana. Mama Masai seemed to know everything that went on in their household. Initially, Wisdom tried hard to satisfy the woman, but found it an increasingly hopeless task. She now merely conversed with her Mother-In-Law with respectful reserve.

"It is different here Mama." Masai explained. "American women are not accustomed to being limited to domestic chores. She just needs time to adjust to me, that is all."

"You should have married a Kenyan girl. I always knew an American wife would be trouble." She huffed a grunt of disgust.

"I'm sure over time you'll like her. You just need to get to know her."

"It is an embarrassment! Wanjeru called me and told me you are skin and bones! She doesn't even cook for you! And worse, you cook for her! Whoever heard of such nonsense?"

His mother was nearing hysterical. *Now I have managed to upset both my mother and my wife,* he thought to himself. He hoped things would get easier.

Wisdom was also on the receiving end of marital advice.

"He seems pretty cooperative if you ask me." Lawana was passing Wiz a cup of tea.

"I don't know, Wana. One minute he is great, and the next he is insane. He can be very gentle and affectionate, even cooks most days. Then he can be chauvinistic and inflexible." Wiz seemed exasperated. Iyana suckled quietly at her mother's breast while the women talked.

"Well, you'll just have to decide what is more important. Your family or your ego." With that, Lawana gave a light chuckle. "I'm sure

Masai's intent is not to have you abandon your dreams completely. Plus, you have to understand that he was raised to think his manhood hangs on his ability to provide for you. In his mind, he must get his degree quickly and provide a stable financial environment. Then, he'd feel more secure and have more room for you to follow your dreams more fully."

"Well, I'm glad to see that you know my husband so well." Wisdom said with a healthy dose of sarcasm.

"I'm just sayin'. Look at it from his perspective sometimes. And stop trippin', damn!"

When the summer came, Wisdom took advantage of the break in school while Masai worked at a print shop in nearby Maryland. The tension eased a bit during this brief pause in Wisdom's schooling. Masai appreciated her willingness to forego summer classes at least. She decided to cook a few times a week as a peace offering, but was careful not to do too much for fear of him starting to expect it. He took some classes over the summer, however to accelerate his pace to graduation.

They tried to plan the second pregnancy to come after Masai graduated, but missed the target a little. The very next year Fumari was born 2 months before Masai's graduation. Wisdom was still in her third year of college and starting to apply to medical schools. Now with a newborn son and young daughter, it was becoming more difficult to manage mothering, school and being a wife. She studied Biochemistry, Neurophysiology, Organic Chemistry, and Human Anatomy. She had survived the highest hurdles on the road to medical school: lack of sleep, demanding professors, constant studying and long hours and had done fairly well. She felt accomplished and satisfied.

"Mother offered to take the children for a few years while you finish your studies." Masai was proud of his wife's accomplishments and glad that his mother had offered this much needed help.

He was now working as an Engineer for the District of Columbia, but had put in an application for a better job near San Francisco since he knew his wife would be applying for medical school there.

"Take the children?" Wisdom was in disbelief at the statement.

Masai was puzzled by her response and obvious displeasure.

"Yes. It's common in our country for children to be sent to live with grandparents for some time. Especially when the parents get very busy and need help."

"No. Absolutely not Masai. I am not comfortable with that. The children will stay with us."

"I don't see how we could possibly raise them properly if you still plan to go to medical school. They can come back when you are done."

"We'll manage. I'm sure of it. They are not going anywhere."

The conversation had ended.

Wisdom would now begin the tasks of acquiring various recommendation letters, taking standardized exams and braving personal interviews for admission into medical school. When the call came from the University of California, College of Medicine that she had been accepted, she was delighted. The same day came with another bit of news as well.

"Fantastic! I knew you could do it!" Masai was grinning from ear to ear and squeezing his wife with news of her acceptance into medical school. "When do you start?"

"August. That's 4 months from now. What about your job? Will you know about the new position by then?"

"I think so, maybe even before. I have to start flying to California to look for an apartment for us all in the meantime. It's going to be a little tough with two kids, you know?"

"Three." Wisdom was calm and waited for Masai to respond.

"Three?" His face was blank.

He sat quiet for a longtime. She knew this news was stressful for him in this moment.

They had agreed after Fumari's birth, that the third child would come after medical school. But since that agreement, Wisdom had thought better of it and had tried to re-visit the topic several times. She thought the earlier the better. Her husband did not agree. Masai, in her mind, was being stubborn because she would not agree to send the children to his mother while she was in medical school. After much begging and pleading, he had reluctantly agreed. He was now reminded of that moment of weakness.

University of California

Kikumbe was born during Wisdom's first year in medical school. Masai had successfully continued his engineering career after accompanying his pregnant wife and two children to California. In addition to his full-time employment, he initially performed as the mother, cook, maid, and nanny, all while supporting Wiz emotionally and otherwise. She was exhausted constantly and when she wasn't studying or taking call in the hospital, she was passed out on the sofa – usually without even undressing or taking off her shoes. Masai would often undress her and carry his exhausted wife to bed after putting the children down for the night. Sex had become scarce, and he missed even having simple conversations with her.

Without much protest, Masai convinced Wisdom to allow one of his elder aunts to move in and help with the house and the children. He could not keep juggling that many roles, nor did he want to. Wiz for one, loved how Masai supported her and she felt guilty that she was not able to give much back. Wisdom realized that although she was not able to provide much to her husband, he was certainly deserving of the warm meals and clean house his aunt provided. The children loved "Auntie" as well, and she took good care of them. Wisdom was climbing up the majestic mountain she has always admired as a child, and Masai climbed by her side over every rock and uneven surface. She promised herself that she'd make it up to him somehow, later on.

"It has been a long while since you travelled home nephew." Auntie was standing at the stove stirring a pot of stew. The house smelled heavenly and Masai was hungry.

"I know Auntie. Mama must have been talking to you about it. I told her we would come when Wisdom was finished with her schooling. Don't fret".

"Yes, it is true she wants to see her son and grandchildren. Can you blame her? Besides, your brother longs to see you as well." She gave a quick glance sideways, and turned to wipe her hands on the towel by the sink.

"Karanga has been angry with me ever since I left to come to America. I'm sure he doesn't miss me much."

"Don't be so sure nephew. Time has a way of changing things." She put a hot bowl of food in front of him.

"How is he anyway? What of his family?" He sipped at the soup spoon carefully.

"All is well. He is aging gracefully and has two beautiful daughters with Wambui. He travels alot. Maybe he'll visit you instead eh?" She amused herself and gave a deep chuckle.

"We'll see. I'll probably beat him to it. I think Wisdom would actually like it there." He was now smiling. Memories of his childhood floated past like mist.

Wisdom's locker at school was not full of the typical student gear. Heavy with her third child, she kept a gas mask to wear in the anatomy lab. The formaldehyde was nauseating, and she was sure the fumes would mutate her growing child.

Time to pump. It's 3 o'clock.

She would take her breast pump into the student lounge to pump milk for her infant son, while trying to make a grocery list for her husband.

As she dissected Emma's lower leg – she often named her cadavers, it made things more personal – she remembered she forgot to put chicken on the list.

Must add chicken. And spaghetti.

Emma still had on the nail polish from the day she had died, at age 82.

Oh yea, and paint for Iyana's room.

Wisdom Masters, M.D. Now she was at the end of a long road, stepping out onto her life's platform, to heal, to fight, to create change.

Chapter 3: Damu

Oakland, California

Wiz was washing that last of the dinner dishes. Masai was putting the children to bed, telling stories of growing up in Kenya and tucking each child into bed carefully. _He is a good father,_ Wiz thought happily as she wiped down the table and the countertops. He quietly crept up behind her and grabbed her tightly around her waist from behind. Chaka Khan was singing "Sweet Thing" to the now serene room as they rocked slowly together, breathing in each others contentment.

"Remember we have a long day tomorrow." Masai reminded Wiz.

"I know, it shouldn't be that bad."

It was Friday night and they planned to drive to Los Angeles early in the morning to visit some of his family.

He was good that way – always remembering to keep in touch with them. Many of his aunts, uncles, cousins, nieces, and nephews were here in the states. His father had passed on, but his mother and his younger brothers were all still in Kenya. Masai didn't speak of them much, didn't even know them all that well really, Wiz thought. She knew that he had spent a lot of his younger years in boarding schools and would see them only occasionally growing up. The brother he spoke of most was Karanga. They were closest in age. He told Wiz that he thought Karanga was careless and too aggressive for his own good. To Wisdom, Masai didn't seem close to his brothers. She thought it was strange to not be close to your own brothers, but she never forced the subject. The rest of his family was pleasant enough, and she loved the fact that the children were multi-lingual because of his family's influence.

She turned to kiss her husband goodnight.

"Come to bed and get some sleep baby." Masai whispered to Wiz.

The slow, warm kiss lingered on her mouth for a while and she agreed to retreat with him for the night.

The two of them walked upstairs to their bedroom. There they retreated to a deep satisfying sleep. At some point in the early hours of the morning, something awakened Wisdom. There was no noise, no nightmares exactly. Her eyes just opened as if she was expecting someone. She slid out of bed, careful not to wake her husband, and walked downstairs to start a pot of tea.

Why couldn't she sleep? *Must be the excitement of seeing family we haven't seen in a few years,* she thought to herself.

After her tea, she washed out the mug she had used and headed back up the stairs. Her steps were interrupted by a soft knock at the door. Not wanting to wake anyone in the house, she looked through the peephole, but didn't say a word. It was Shug. Why would he be there? Although their relationship was not sexual and purely innocent then, he usually didn't come to her home around her family. They were mere acquaintances, not even considered friends really. This was highly unusual. Unless… it was urgent. She knew it must be urgent.

She opened the door, and put her finger to his lips, encouraging him to be absolutely silent. Another man was with Shug, holding him up even, and Shug's entire shirt was soaked in blood.

"He's been shot Wisdom. He's been bleeding real bad" the young man said. "He wouldn't let me take him to the hospital, 'cause he's on parole and they'd put him back in jail for good. It's his third strike, ya' know. He said to bring him to you. He knew you'd take care of him."

Shug was barely conscious he had lost so much blood.

Wisdom's mind was racing now. What should she do? Where should she start?

Over the years, she had transformed her basement into a make-shift delivery room for pregnant women. The government had gotten to the point that women were in dangers of loosing their babies for a variety of different reasons. So many African-American newborns were wards of the state and in foster care. Reason's for having a child removed from one's custody after delivery at the hospital could include suspected drug use, cigarette smoking, suspected alcoholic abuse, victims of domestic violence, carriers of any number of infectious diseases like HIV, gonorrhea or syphilis, or even history of a chronic illness. Any prison record or probation history was also grounds for infant-mother separation. So many women were attempting unsafe deliveries elsewhere without proper care.

This eventually forced Wisdom to open her doors as a community service even wider. As such, she had equipped her "clinic" with basic medical supplies: sutures, scissors, scalpels, clamps, basic anesthesia, IV bags, oxygen tanks, a few antibiotics and simple first aid supplies. Never was she presented with a real trauma situation, and her only choice was to improvise.

"I'm Phil, by the way." The young man said as he struggled to assist Shug.

"Hi Phil. Ok, take him down to the basement, the door should be open. Lie him down

on the exam table down there and take his shirt off.
I'll be right down." Wisdom was rattling off
instructions as she rehearsed in her mind what she
needed to do.

She grabbed some morphine from her
locked cabinet in the kitchen - she had started
keeping certain drugs in the house after a few
robberies in the basement – and some garlic extract
from the refrigerator. She tied back her hair and ran
down to where the two men were waiting. She
quickly started and IV into Shug's arm, handed the
bag of fluid to Phil and told him to squeeze the bag
as hard as he could while holding it high in the air
so that fluid would flow quickly.

After slapping an oxygen mask onto Shug's
face, she cleaned with iodine the area where the
blood seemed to be gushing most rapidly. *There is
not exit wound on his body, so the bullet must still
be inside,* she thought. It had entered in his front
left shoulder and was too deep to see.

"Here, stick this needle into this tube and
push this liquid in slowly." Wiz handed Phil a
syringe of morphine. "I have to reach into the
wound and locate the bullet."

After torching the clamp with a lighter, she
clamped the blood vessel that seemed to be bleeding
most, and carefully guided another inside the wound
beside her finger. When she could feel the hard

object just beneath, she opened the clamp, grasped the bullet and carefully guided it out. Luckily it was still whole, and not in a million pieces. She released the other clamped off of the blood vessel, and packed the wound with gauze soaked in garlic extract.

"Hold pressure right here on the wound, I'll be right back." Wiz ran upstairs to start some barley soup and ginger tea.

Wiz and Phil took turns spoon-feeding Shug all night. The bleeding had stopped and Shug's blood pressure and pulse were normalizing.

"It's about five in the morning and I have to leave." Wiz was nervous about leaving the men unattended, but needed time to go check on her family.

"Come get me if anything changes. Me and the family will probably leave for L.A. in a few hours, so once we leave you should move him into the guest room upstairs."

Phil was listening intently. "What do you mean if anything changes?"

"If this bandage soaks with blood or if you cannot wake him up, stuff like that." Phil's eyes widened. "Here, I'll also show you how to take his blood pressure and his pulse and I'll right down what is normal. Call me if either becomes abnormal." Wiz gave Phil a smile of encouragement. "I'll come down a few times before we leave to check on him."

"He is to drink only the soup and tea I made and to chew raw garlic five times a day to prevent infection." Phil was now taking notes. "God willing, he'll survive the night."

"You can contact me by phone while I am away. You both should be gone by the time we get back from L.A. on Sunday night at nine o'clock."

Then she ran upstairs, showered, and helped Masai ready the children for the trip.

The night's events were stressful but exhilarating and Wiz's mind was still racing. She thought of Shug the entire ride to Southern California, during her visit there and entire ride back to Oakland. When she got home, there was a message on the answering machine from Peaches, Shug's mother, saying that she had received the pound of sugar that Wiz had sent over, and she appreciated her kindness and generosity. Wisdom was relieved to know that Shug was alright, and that the entire ordeal was over. But that one incident got the word out quietly, and over the next several years, Wiz's basement clinic serviced anyone from pregnant mothers to gunshot and stab wound victims, abused and battered women, broken bones, scrapes, and bruises.

Wiz welcomed anyone and developed a skill for both guerilla and herbal medicine. The community considered her clinic a place of solitude and healing, one that even the critically injured or sick, with no hope of recovery, chose to come to before they died. The community had started a burial fund for fallen men and women, headed by Shug. When people with no hope of survival from their assorted injuries chose not to suffer and die in a hospital, surrounded by uniformed officers and sterile doctors, they could come to Wisdom and make their transition "at home". Wiz would climb into a warm bathtub with her "patient", she wearing a swimsuit and the patient dressed in whatever was comfortable. She would burn sage and sing or hum songs of freedom into their ears. She would bathe them, wash their hair, caress their dying bodies and allow them to ride her energy back to the ancestors. Witnesses to these flights swore they saw the deceased spirits as Wisdom guided them back into the sky.

Auntie was Wisdom's trusted assistant in the clinic as well as the house. When Masai learned of the first death in the clinic, it was Auntie who soothed his mind and calmed his fears.

"It's too much Auntie. Such things should not be allowed to happen around the children." Masai was afraid for his wife and the attention it was bringing to their household.

"It is women's work Masai. Birth and Death. It is raw and real, no veils to soften it or useless noise to drown it out. It is what she lives to do. Let her live. I'll manage the children."

And so it was.

In her work, Wiz always felt satisfied, powerful, and at the same time, sad and worried during her work at the basement clinic. But, it balanced her work at the small government clinic during the weekdays. Old, used equipment, along with outdated protocols made that work more exhausting than satisfying. Seemingly endless lines of patients, in search of medicine and comfort crowded the small waiting room at the Uptown Women's Clinic, which often smelled of mold and dust. Still, it was a steady income and helped contribute to soothing the disease of the community.

Chapter 4: Foundations

Oakland, California

He was a junior, named for his father and later would live for him as well. The little man, with bounding heart and fists of energy. He thought circles around his lighter counterparts in grade school and was labeled "mischievous" by teachers and caregivers. He was unable to be confined, never coerced or manipulated. In fact, Wisdom's brother Rakim was always a leader and the decision maker among his friends. He earned the nickname "Sergeant", later shortened to "Sarg." As he aged, he had tried his hand at drug sales, gun trading, petty theft at local department stores and suffered countless trips to jail as a teen – each time with a resolve to create an even more tactical, fool proof plan the next time.

Growing up, Sarg was mesmerized by his father's talk of African revolution, Black History and the ancestors, and was always ashamed of ending up in jail- right where the "White Man" wanted him. Nobody made his shame burn more than his sister Wisdom.

"If you want to beat the 'White Man' Sarg, you have to out smart him. Selling drugs to your community, shooting and killing other members of the community is just not smart. It's counter productive." Wisdom had always hoped her brother would settle down into a more conventional life.

"I know Wiz. I am not the type to sit in office all day, nor go to college. Opportunities are limited." He knew she would not accept that as an excuse.

"Then start your own business. A *legitimate* business. You already have some of the skills necessary. You understand supply and demand, consumer habits, marketing and even profit margins. You just need to find a better product. One that is not so destructive."

"Just because something is legal does not make it less destructive. Look at tobacco and alcohol for example."

"You're right. The question you have to ask yourself is what mark you want to leave on the world and the community when you leave. On your family. Destruction happens at the consumer level, it happens at the community level if it encourages violence and discourages unity, it happens at the family level when children are missing parents who are locked up for illegal activity. By opening a legal business, you at least eliminate the last two. You have to decide for yourself just like any other business person if the product you decide to sell will be harmful or not."

Despite his desire to be free, Sarg remained a frequent guest to the correctional facilities, and hungered for better control over his destiny. When a Pan African National Alliance (PANA) supporter first approached him in prison, his mind was fertile for planting, his spirit eager to fly. It was known to all that most of the inmates in the maximum security isolation unit or 'the hole', were members of PANA.

PANA was a global organization, based in East Africa. There, it was called the Alliance. The focus was the unification of African nations, including those African descendants in the diaspora, for the liberation from neocolonial rule, promotion of independence and development and the overall betterment of everyday life. It's base was in East Africa because since the political enlightenment of the 1960's when multiple African nations won their independence almost simultaneously, several African nations united to form one large nation. Kenya, Tanzania, and Uganda had merged currencies, governments and militaries, creating a united African state. This transformation had tipped the balance of power from dependence on European economic and military aide, with it's nourishment of European companies and interests, to independence and the pivot away from subsidizing European economies. The transformation had also at once created instant enemies including the European Union, the

American CIA, as well as The World Bank and the International Monetary Fund. The agency these entities used to covertly fight African unification and independence was Interpol, the International Police, along with endless numbers of private mercenaries for hire. With the broader African Liberation Movement raging forward, of which PANA was a critical player, the stage was set for a classic war of the worlds.

In prison, PANA members preached Socialism, African Unity and political education. Some saw them as an over-aged bunch of drug addicts, still trying to live the the 1960's dream. Sarg liked them. They had an ideology and a purpose, always resisting the status quo in prison and trying to educate the younger cats. They were bold.

"What's up young blood?" a PANA leader named Askari whispered to Sarg from the other side of the adjacent wall.

Sarg had been sent to the hole many times for fighting in the population, but this was the first time a PANA officer had attempted any kind of contact.

"You know OG, same old bullshit." Sarg replied.

"It's only the same because you let it be."

Silence.

"Whatever, man." Sarg sounded disgusted. "I suppose you can control when they lock your ass up in this hole huh?"

"Of course. Can't you?"

"Don't fuck with me man!"

Sarg was convinced that Askari was strikingly ignorant. His anger with the entire conversation twirled him into a frenzy of scattered thoughts and climbing rage.

Askari too, felt the building tension, and thus ended the conversation. He would not contact Sarg again for seven days, and his next greeting was less provocative.

Askari gave short, specific instructions.

"When the guard comes with the next meal tray, there will be three pages from a book hidden underneath. Read them. If you'd like to know more, you will receive three pages a day until you've completed the book." That was all he said.

Sarg could hear Askari's movements from over the wall between their two prison cells. Sarg heard Askari rise every morning at 4 AM and complete two full hours of what sounded like very strenuous exercise. He later found out that the whispers he often heard from the adjacent wall where a combination of daily meditations and Swahili lessons Askari would practice to himself. He slowly started asking Askari questions regarding the book he was continuing to read, as well as sharing his thoughts on the subject.

Sarg spent 90 days in the hole this way, learning from Askari. Sarg was sent to the hole anytime he engaged in any fighting, which was often. By the time he was re-integrated back into the main population, he had read *How Europe Underdeveloped Africa*, by Walter Rodney, *The Art of War*, by Sun Tzu, and *Soledad Brother*, by George Jackson. He would schedule regular incidents to return to the hole and "go to school".

When the news came that Askari and two other PANA veterans had been assassinated while in the hole, Shaka knew he would have to reach Sarg quickly and quietly. Shaka was a senior leader and organizer in PANA and had learned from Askari that Sarg had the heart of a lion, the patience of a drug addict and was bound to react foolishly. He was too valuable a warrior to loose to the prison labyrinth. Shaka arranged a visit to the prison to give information on university registration for soon-to-be- released inmates. He knew Sarg's release date was in six months, and Shaka had put on the underground PANA wire in the prison that any and all PANA members were to take advantage of this educational opportunity.

The temperature was rising inside the prison for PANA members, near boiling. The recent attempt to destroy the political uprising with serial murders of active members was an old and now infective method of subjugation used by Interpol and it's allies. Shaka knew that any rushed political or military response would mean severe consequences for those on the inside. Plans were firmly in place to remove two of the remaining PANA veterans in one week, and he needed Sarg to remain discrete and focused.

When Sarg approached the desk, after an exhaustive wait in line, he was underwhelmed by Shaka's presence. Shaka wore a beige, linen, short-sleeved button down shirt, over baggy legged linen pants and navy blue cloth shoes. He had long, flowing locks and wore tinted sunglasses. *This guy is too polished to be a supposed "comrade,"* Sarg thought suspiciously. He was skeptical and cautious with his words towards this stranger.

"Hey man, how you doin'?"

Shaka was handing Sarg a registration packet, and peering over the top of his handsome glass frames. "Peace brother."

"Sign your name and release date here, and fill out the top from in you packet title 'PFCF Registration'".

Sarg took the packet over to a cold, gray table and identified the form. *Who is this cat anyway?* He carefully surveyed each blank to be completed: Name: <u>Rakim Masters</u>. DOB: <u>1/13/73</u>. Field of Anticipated Study: <u>Science of Politics.</u> Curious. All sections had been filled in already. He gave a quick glance over to the man at the registration desk, and then proceeded.

Address: <u>142 Underpass.</u> Also filled in. After completing the other few blank spaces remaining, he returned the packet to the man at the desk.

"Thank you, young man. Can I answer any questions for you?" Shaka asked in a light tone.

"No, Sir. I think I understand everything."

"Good then. See you when you get out. Be sure to stop by my office when it's that time."

They parted without saying anything further. Sarg was disturbed by these instructions to lay low. Surely the slaying of top PANA officers must have boundless and consuming repercussions. *There must be a bigger plan*, he wondered. *Better to lay low now and wait for further instructions.* But when two nights later, the two remaining PANA veterans in the hole were reported to have escaped, Sarg felt betrayed and excluded. He should have been let in on the breakout, been involved in the orchestration or at least execution of the operation. While huge steps were being made in the struggle, monumental blows for freedom, he was sound asleep on his bunk in the cool, damp concrete cell. What had he been doing all this work for, if not to fight for the salvation of his people? It was an insult, and when his time was served, he'd present his frustrations to the clean, pressed gentleman from whom he received the insult.

It was prison policy to keep the veteran members of PANA secluded from the general population for fear of "over education" and incitement of political riots. PANA was categorized as a gang by prison authorities, and as such was subject to the same scrutiny: limiting contact and movement between members. Despite the purposeful attempts to prevent cooperation and coordination between he and his comrades, Sarg thrived as a junior member and eventually an officer in PANA.

Over the 6 years he spent in prison under the teachings of PANA, he attained both physical and mental agility and hungered for knowledge as if it were his only sustenance. He learned fluent Swahili and became versed in ancient African philosophy, international economics and politics. He later grew into his name 'Sarg' even more fully. Whereas before, it was like a shirt a few sizes too big, now it fit perfect in all the right places and felt like his natural skin. He moved well in it and it was comfortable. It was here, in the confines of prison walls and dulled senses, that he would meet Bird, who later turned out to be a lifelong friend and confidant.

Word was in the joint that one of the members of a southern gang had decided to pull out. He had been a lifelong member, as was his father and uncles before him. He had a reputation for being one of the best, most enduring fighters in prison. No man could even touch him. So when word spread that Bird wanted out, excitement grew behind the tall thick walls in anticipation of the coming events. Everyone knew that leaving this gang was prohibited, punishable by death. Multiple members of the gang were obligated to beat the identified traitor until he ceased to breathe. But with Bird, the task would be a great one. Sarg was lying on his bunk reading when a stampede rumbled down the hall. *Must be the main event,* he thought to himself. But he continued his studies, only later to be interrupted again, this time by a new young PANA recruit, Malik.

"Ain't you gone do somethin' man? They tryin' to kill Bird!"

"Why should I?" Sarg asked. "That gang shit is so stupid and self-destructive. Why should I risk my fuckin' life to get involved in that dumb shit?"

"Because PANA is the reason he wants to stop bangin."

Sarg sat up, listening more intently.

"I've been talkin' to dude. A little anyway. He's my cellie."

Sarg jumped off his bunk and ran toward the now swelling crowd. "Why didn't you say that at the beginning?"

When Sarg pushed his way through the crowd, Bird's face was swollen beyond recognition. His hands and mouth were bloody from fighting. He was still standing though, and no doubt would have fought to the death had Sarg not stepped in.

"You sure you want to do that, blood?" one of the gang members said with a threatening tone.

It was known that interfering in internal gang relations was not tolerated from outsiders and a risk of endangerment would surely follow.

"I think young blood had had enough. Besides he Fam now." Fam, short for family, had become the popular name for members of PANA.

"Did you think I'd let this go all the way?" Sarg continued. "He's had enough practice for one day."

Sarg looked his challenger in the eye and smiled slowly. The other three men were off to the side wounded and weak. Bird was definitely a soldier and would be an asset to the organization and to the movement if he chose to joint the ranks.

Bird spent the next week in the prison infirmary receiving care for his battle wounds. While recovering, he sent Sarg a "kite" thanking him and requesting his lessons begin as soon as possible. Kites were underground written messages containing classified information that were smuggled amongst inmates. His request was granted immediately.

Sarg took Bird under his wing and educated him personally. He was a quick learner and fierce competitor. He never swayed in his loyalty to PANA or to Sarg and never hesitated to carry out an order, no matter how small or large. Bird was just as eager to accomplish small tasks, such as completing a selected reading list, as he was to fill larger orders like physically enforcing PANA security. Sarg liked Bird inside and out and took pride in his eager, young recruit. He trusted Bird with his life, time and time again, and was never the least bit disappointed. He would later trust him with the lives of countless others.

Over time, Bird got to know about Wisdom from Sarg's narratives inside the prison walls. His loyalty to Sarg quickly extended to the entire family before any of them even know he existed. He was dedicated to learning from and protecting the patriarch, Pops: he felt a sense of responsibility toward Abu, Dubane and Modoe and he swore to defend and protect Wisdom.

Sarg had shown Bird pictures of Wisdom and read passages from her letters , flowing with warmth and knowledge. She was a simple woman on the photographs, by no means an overwhelming beauty or sex symbol. She was fully clothed, head wrapped with no makeup. Ordinary features and serene, happy expressions. But her voice in the letters brought a life to the pictures that was bright and blinding. Since he had a wife and children on the outside, he sometimes felt guilty for being so hypnotized by her. Bird listened to her often, through those readings with Sarg. He even imagined whole dialogues with her.

What we focus on becomes our reality, Wiz would say in a letter.

Our minds are infinite and limitless.

She would encourage education and meditation. She would also give advice about diet and exercise.

Life is Motion. Never stop moving.

He was proud of her, as if she was his own sister, and he worried her worries and wanted to calm her fears. In his mind, he carried her over mountains and lifted her from dark, deep seas. Over the course of three years in prison with Sarg, Bird formed a deep and lasting relationship with Wisdom. He loved her and would kill and die for her. And Wiz hadn't the slightest clue who he was.

Sarg was careful about revealing any political agendas or personal connections in his correspondences with Wiz from prison. He had always spoken openly with her when he was on the outside, but knew that discretion while behind enemy lines was crucial to survival. All mail was monitored.

Sarg first introduced Wiz to Bird to a few months after he was released from prison. Bird had been out two months prior, and Sarg asked Wisdom if she wouldn't mind accompanying him to a friend's house, whose pregnant wife was sick. She wouldn't go to the hospital because she didn't trust white doctors. He knew Wisdom could never say no to a woman in need. He explained that the friend's name was Bird, and that he had been Sarg's cellmate in prison for the last few years.

"He's like a brother to me, Wiz." Sarg had explained. "I'm only asking because he's worried about her."

Wisdom agreed and was pleasantly surprised to meet this beautiful, soft-eyed brother. She learned from Sarg on the ride over that Bird was an ex-gang member from L.A., and had spend a lot of his life in jail for a number of felonies. She was all ready to meet some musty, overweight brother with a Snoop Dog perm, wearing a tight "wife beater" t-shirt hugging his shining chest, as he bench pressed two Rottweilers, pausing occasionally to shine his gold teeth. Instead, when Bird answered the door with his five year-old son was in his arms, all stereotypes were crushed in Wisdom's mind. He was so happy and relieved to greet his friend finally on the outside, that he grabbed Sarg in a tight embrace with such intense emotion that Wisdom almost started to cry.

"Hey Man, this is my sister Wiz." Sarg was beaming with pride.

Bird extended his hand, "Wow, nice to meet you Sis. I've heard alot of good things about you. My name is Donald, but everybody calls me Bird." His smile lingered in the air.

"Hi Bird, nice to meet you too." She shook his extended hand and smiled politely.

After their greeting, Wiz was able to get a better look at him.

Bird was about six feet tall, medium build and dark brown skin. His perfect lemon drop eyes were in sharp contrast to his firm, tight jaw line. His perfectly chiseled, lean body was evident even under his modest attire. She warmed under his careful touch and watched as he and her brother openly enjoyed their reunion.

The remaining part of the afternoon, Wiz spent talking to Bird's wife, Dasia and helping with her two small children. She was full with a new life and due to deliver any day. She was feeling slow and tired, the usual end of pregnancy fatigue – but nothing more. Wiz was confused about why all the concern on Bird's part. Surely his wife had experienced similar feelings with the first two pregnancies. She was proud of what a dedicated father he was and ashamed of her previous assumptions about him. He was just beautiful. Beautiful in every way, and she accepted him quickly as a new member to the family.

Wisdom was summoned several more times over the coming months to assist Dasia with this task or another. She slowly grew to know not only Bird, but his wife and children. Dasia was clear about her disapproval of his involvement in PANA and took every opportunity to express her disdain.

"He finds every excuse to be away from us, our family. First it was gangs, then prison, now this ridiculous 'army'. If you ask me, it's just another gang really." Dasia sounded defeated in her protest.

"This is different." Wiz said back slowly, with feeling. "There is a purpose here, with a positive outcome if we are successful. For *all* of our people." Wisdom couldn't understand why any woman wouldn't support such a stance.

"*We* should be his purpose!" Dasia insisted, and she slowly moved her hand over her distended belly. "What good is ensuring a positive outcome for strangers and ignoring your family?"

"Maybe he needs that to feel useful to society, to be seen as a good leader of your family."

"Maybe." Dasia said, as she let out a long sigh.

She liked that Wisdom always tried to get her to see the other perspective, but at the same time Wisdom, as a woman and mother, also understood her frustration.

Chapter 5: The Mark

Oakland, California

The movement had been building momentum in the hearts and minds of the local people. Gone were the days of peaceful protests and political rallies. The people saw the police as a giant force pressing against the underclass, to enforce mass oppression and confusion. Now the people were pushing back. Men and women no longer bowed to the siren of a pursuing police car. High-speed chases and shoot-outs were as common as traffic lights in the hood. Everybody had a "lick" or scam in the works to supplement whatever insufficient income was paid by their regular jobs. People felt underpaid and overworked. Elderly folk had scams as well- welfare or foster care fraud, insurance scams or prescription drug sales.

The people felt they had very little to lose and everything to gain from organizing a retaliation in response to rampant violence against their communities. Every brotha in the neighborhood was either out on bail, on parole or in between jail stretches. Many had fathered several children during brief episodes of freedom, and most of the children were later left fatherless, feeling abandoned. Slave labor had been reborn through the prison system, with many of America's corporate giants contracting prison labor for little to nothing. The free labor force was kept bountiful by legislation aimed at ensuring frequent and prolonged trips to jail of any man or woman of color in poverty. The freedom movement in the Black community was now awakening from a long slumber, refreshed and energized, flexing its muscles as it stretched and yawned, ready for the new day, ready to create and re-claim its destiny.

Wisdom saw it swelling with infinite power and energy. She knew it would need direction, and hoped she would be able to have even a small role within it. During high school, college and even medical school, she had been aware of her role, and had been involved in a gamut of different African organizations from the Black Students Union, to Pan African Unions, from African socialist movements to history and cultural societies. She had engaged in countless conversations about the "revolution" with friends, co-workers, lovers and her parents, but none as passionate as the exchanges with her brother, Sarg.

He had gone into prison as a teen. He had been an angry, confused man-child, and emerged a soldier in the Pan African National Alliance (PANA). He would speak with such zeal and force on any topic pertaining to freedom and self-determination for African people. He would glow with electricity as he and Wiz debated strategies, discussed philosophy and revealed opinions about the primary objective of revolution.

Wisdom knew that these where the times when her brother had overcome his shame and guilt about prison, and she always tried to make him know how proud she was of him, and that she was aware of his brilliance. He would occasionally hint on the ideology and his role in PANA, but never in great detail, for security reasons. In one debate, they had each acknowledged the recent surge in the movement, and Sarg confided that the cadre of his party were going to hold one of the most important meetings in their history, and he was responsible for the logistics and security of the event.

"It's happening Wiz. The people are tired of unemployment, chronic poverty and police brutality. We have no food, no way to provide food, no medical care, no education. Most of our men spend an average of seven to ten years in prison over their lifetime. The streets are hot right now-people just don't give a fuck! If a brotha don't have food or money, he takin' that shit! No car? Go take one! Brothas is swingin' back now, and hard! Police think twice about pullin' us over unless they got major backup! High-speed chases, shoot outs ... the people not down with this bullshit no more! My comrades are ready to redirect all this defiant energy into a monster movement! Never before have conditions been this ripe!"

Sarg was electric in his delivery. Wisdom was admittedly excited by the speech and agreed.

"You're right! It's time for the leaders in our communities to direct mass action. But most of our organizations are impotent, and don't carry the trust nor loyalty of the people."

"Except PANA!" Sarg insisted. "We are actively recruiting and training young men and women as soldiers in the African liberation and succeeding! We have over one million active members worldwide and continuing to grow!"

Wisdom listened intently.

"The problem is, the Man is hip to the game and it is becoming more difficult to meet, plan and organize without being sabotaged by some kind of counterintelligence."

"You must be a pretty formidable group if you incite government counter tactics. Man, I had no idea!" Wisdom confessed with sincere awe.

"Of course you didn't. The middle and upper classes have been, until now, purposely excluded from our activity for fear of betrayal. But now, the organization has called for an international meeting of the twelve elders to discuss strategies and timing of both offensive and defensive operations within the movement. This is where you come in Wiz."

"Where *I* come in?! Sarg, what are you trying to get me into?" she said with a smirk. "I thought me and 'my kind' were not to be trusted. You know, no secret safe with me and my money." Her tone was sarcastic, the whole while trying to camouflage how insulted she felt by his prior comments over the years.

"Yes, but now we must open our minds and include all. African people in the fight against oppression come in all flavors. After-all, we are all affected to an extent. Besides, it's the perfect cover! Who expects Black folk with a little change to jeopardize everything for their poorer brothas and sistahs? Nobody! That is, nobody with a capitalist's mind, anyway."

Wisdom continued to wonder. "Okay, say that is true. Some may be willing to sacrifice, but others will not. How will you identify willing parties without exposing yourself to the wrong people?"

"I don't have to. You will."

"Here you go with that me shit again! I don't know anything or anyone in your group. What makes you think they'll trust me with any information?"

"I trust you. That's all anyone will need. First things first. Remember when I told you earlier that a big meeting has been called?"

"Yes, the elders or something."

"Well, I'm responsible for organizing the place, time and appropriate security. It needs to be held at a spot not affiliated with any underground politics. I'm hoping you'll agree to let us use your place."

"Is that all? Of course you guys can meet here." She was relieved that the request was so modest.

"I'm glad. I figured it would be okay since the children and Masai will be in Kenya and won't be here during those few days. Oh, and everyone will be arriving from out of town and will need overnight accommodations. Is that okay?"

"Days? How many days? And why *can't* my family be here?"

"Four days. We need time to discuss and plan major modes of action. There is also potential for police raids and violence. So, children and non-involved parties are never allowed to attend."

Wisdom had believed that for all this time, she had been dedicated to the cause. Now, she couldn't help wondering what she had just gotten herself into. How deeply would her involvement be?

She was nervous for the first time, almost sorry she had agreed. She should have discussed this with Masai before agreeing. Would he even allow it? How should she tell him? Would her children be in danger afterward? Would she be sworn to loyalty to this group now and risk death if she withdrew? It was too late now. She had given her word to her baby brother, and she knew he trusted her with his life. How could she change her mind now?

Sarg had told her stories of his "Baba's" Askari and Shaka, the ones who taught him and embraced him into the brotherhood of PANA. Shaka sounded solid, father-like, and strong. Wiz was not usually intrigued by older men, but her interest in this one was perking. She could feel by Sarg's description that Shaka was principled, intelligent and loyal to her brother. She liked him and even felt close to him in a strange way. She had not even met him yet. But soon she would.

Chapter 6: The Call

Ngong Hills, Nairobi, Kenya

Karanga Mogi had become one of the most dangerous men in the world. He headed the formidable East African Alliance, the recent union of Kenya, Ethiopia, Eritrea and Tanzania that was born out of the war against British influence in the region. It was the largest functioning faction of PANA; the first attempt at a united Africa, and it was succeeding. The region had a thriving economy, as well as international trade with alliances such as Libya, Cuba, Angola and China.

The combined military was forceful and enormous. General Mogi was also Shepsu in PANA. His wife Wambui and two teen daughters were under constant guard, and he rarely interacted with non-party members. He was the only one of his line left in Kenya; both parents had long since passed on, and his older brother Masai, also a civil engineer as he was, had moved to the United States years ago and married there. It frustrated him that his brother was so conservative and followed the Western rules, even at the expense of their people. He had not seen nor spoken to his older brother since he abandoned Karanga and their younger brothers in search of a "better life" in the West more than 20 years before. He did however, receive a monthly financial donation from his brother toward the Alliance.

Karanga was in constant correspondence with the other Shepsu in positions to further the immediate cause of the East African Alliance as well as the overall cause of PANA. Shepsu Antonio Bautista of Nicaragua was a weapons and combat specialist. Shepsu Kua Ovambo of Angola ran a biochemistry research laboratory with her husband and partner. Shepsu Hai-Nan Boktang of Cambodia was an economist and expert in international business and trade. All made regularly scheduled visits to Kenya to support the new found independence of their brothers and sisters there.

The Alliance held the same significance of a virtual Zion, a promised land of sorts. It was the symbol of African Unity, power and integrity.

Every African nation and pro-Africa political group in the diaspora pledged allegiance to the united body and sent trained staff to help ensure its survival. Rumor floated of the Alliances attempt to persuade Sudan to be its newest member, but the Western hold on Sudan was strong, and European and American attempts to destabilize the region were habitual. U.S. puppet governments in Sudan and Uganda made civil wars and violent conflict between the two countries almost insurmountable. U.S. intelligence attempts to infiltrate and destroy PANA and the Alliance were also constant, and a surplus of money and man power was spent to merely maintain those bodies as functioning, effective entities.

Karanga traveled often, and his wife Wambui ruled the nation as Queen Mother in his absence. Their two daughters, Shanzu, who was 19 years old, and Thika 17, were fluent in both English and French in addition to their native Swahili and Kikuyu languages. Shanzu had even started to pick up some Arabic and Portuguese in her studies at the university. Both daughters knew the regions politics completely and were versed in, and loyal to the ideology and objective of the Alliance. Shanzu wished to be a professor of international law, and eventually hold a position in PANA, in hopes of shaping the future of the continent, like her father had done. She wore conservative attire most times, preferred air-conditioned buildings and made regular appointments to have her teeth whitened. He hair was straightened, her presence always sharp.

Thika had the fire and resolve of her father however, and wanted to be his successor as General and Chief of the Alliance. Her nails were not manicured. She wore vibrant colors, beads and head wraps reminiscent of her Masai ancestors. Her hair was knotted and curly, her presence always sharp. She held firm opinions on sexism and gender roles in the African community, and challenged even the most senior of her elders on any action toward or belief pertaining to women she deemed inappropriate. Her biggest discussions were with Baba Bautista, the PANA weapons and combat specialist in Nicaragua.

"Your ranks are lacking in women soldiers Comrade Bautista. Why is that?" Thika's piercing stare was as intense as her accusing tone.

"Not lacking young comrade. In fact, we have more women now than ever."

Antonio was clearly amused with Thika.

"Which is shameful indeed, since that still only accounts for less than ten percent of the force." Thika huffed.

"Shameful? No, not really. Women have many roles in society, and choosing to be a soldier effectively eliminates all of their other choices. Not many women desire being limited in that way."

"But why be limited at all? Men are not limited by this choice. Most are soldiers, husbands and fathers. Many are even active community members in times of peace."

"Indeed, you do speak the truth." Antonio was smiling warmly at Thika. He regarded her as he would his own daughters. "I cannot speak for all men, only myself. I choose to be in the military. I choose to leave my wives for endless months at a time, sometimes years, and hope that they will not only survive, but thrive in my absence. I choose to leave my children in the care of their mothers and not participate in the day to day rearing and teaching of any of them. I choose to be an absent parent and spouse. I choose to leave my elderly parents and to not be there to assist and protect them in their final years. I leave that to my siblings. My wives have decided not to make that choice. Even Carla, who I'm sure would no doubt be an excellent soldier. She chooses to stay with the children. She chooses to care for the other women and the elders. I imagine that to be the reason why most women do not choose a life of military adventures. It can be very lonely at times."

Thika thought for a while contemplating her response.

"What *if* more women desired to join the military. Would you encourage or discourage it?" Thika asked.

"Neither. We accept all qualified applicants without making judgements. All that is needed is one's physical and mental strength and dedication to securing freedom for our people."

Antonio Bautista and Thika's father Karanga were very close, and Thika had spent much time with Antonio and his eldest son, Simone. She resented the fact that Antonio had six children by three different women. She had only met Simone, who was 17 years old as she was, and assumed Baba Bautista did not support or parent the others.

Simone had four younger sisters and a baby brother. He was a cocoa-skinned brother with long, straight black hair like the Indians she had seen in old cowboy movies. She thought he looked like Geronimo. He was very attractive, if you liked that type, the exact likeness of his father.

"Why are you so concerned with being a man's physical equal in fighting, shooting and the like? It's a waist of energy really. Maybe you should really be focused more on achieving intellectual and social equality."

What a beautiful body, Simone thought, *to be wasted in combat.*

"We don't need to *achieve* intellectual equality, we are already matched with men in intellect. In fact, I would argue we surpass you in that arena!" *Idiot!*, Thika thought.

Thika was obviously disgusted with Simone's argument. "And yes, social equality is important. But with the current state of the male psyche, women must also be prepared physically to defend themselves. Who's to say men will voluntarily and without malice, agree to social equality for women?"

Thika's eyes burned with passion. She was animated and angry, which excited Simone sexually. He watched her hungrily as she spoke.

"That's is what husbands are for." Simone answered. "Once a woman is married, her husband becomes her protector. Before that, her father. Society has a way to protect women without them raising weapons against their own community." Simone knew his last statement was fuel for Thika's fire.

"You cannot be serious Simone! The exact reason women are not seen as equals now is the bullshit is passed down from fathers to their sons, who later become husbands and fathers. I for one am not waiting until marriage to ensure that I am protected. I can protect myself."

Simone would see to it that Thika's body would not go to waste, and was always protected he thought to himself. Simone planned to have Thika as his wife someday, but would have to be clever and careful or risk being rejected by the General's daughter forever. Simone was extremely articulate, and could debate one into doubting her very own existence. Thika liked their electric debates however, despite the fact that she thought he was an arrogant, sexist asshole. She looked forward to Baba Bautista's visits if only to see Simone and fight once again.

Thika was nearing the end of high school and was preparing to join her sister at the university in the fall, a fate she resisted violently. Shanzu was a lady, she had countless male admirers, and was as crisp as new money. She knew all the right phrases, had perfect etiquette and behavior suitable to a proper Kikuyu woman. She assisted her mother in maintaining the flow of both family and government business. A tributary or diplomat of sorts, she was smooth, inviting and an expert ego tamer and master of redirecting agendas. But Thika knew she wasn't like her sister. And she didn't want to be like that. She was a self-proclaimed militant. She pictured herself in the military, a tactical genius who would make enemies cower in fear and triumph in Africa's fight for freedom. She had no time for dinner parties, meetings or conferences. She never kissed ass, but bit holes in a few.

Thika's doubled edged tongue sliced giants in half. She was abrupt and honest, fierce and relentless. The university was for thinkers, and she was a doer. An argument that did not sway her father.

"I do not wish to waste my time with a bunch of arm-chair revolutionaries father! While the students sit around philosophizing, I can be of more use to you in the field. Let Shanzu go learn how to be a diplomat. I want to train to be a soldier!" Thika was pleading with Karanga.

"No, Thika you are definitely going to finish your studies. Combat training is not even up for discussion or negotiation right now."

"Then when?" Thika responded, clearly defeated.

"We will discuss it again when you finish at the university. One must learn the principles of freedom and justice before one can defend them."

Simone was secretly pleased when she complained of her parent's stubbornness.

"My parents treat me like a child. I am capable and willing, but still they shield me from anything considered dangerous. It would not be so if I were a son." Thika lay on her back looking up to the sky.

A gentle breeze rolled over her causing an eruption of goose-bumps on her flesh. Simone placed his sweater over her arms.

"Well, maybe. I don't know. But at least you'll meet new people at the university. Maybe even some you'll like." Simone teased.

He turned to face her, with his hand holding the side of his face and his body propped up on one elbow.

"Maybe he'll let you come train with my father at the ranch during your breaks. I can even help train you." His grin irritated Thika.

"I should be the one training *you*." Thika threw the sweater over Simone's head and jumped up to run before he could catch her.

Karanga was secretly delighted with Thika's fire, and he never doubted her ability or her resolve-only her discretion. Her ideals would mature at the university with time. Karanga hoped Thika would settle in her ways and become less reactionary. He would however, allow her to spend a few weeks in Nicaragua in Baba Bautista's training camp during breaks from school. He could trust that her safety would be guaranteed with Antonio, as if being guarded personally by Karanga himself.

"Baba Bautista has invited you to train with him on the ranch during your breaks from school." Karanga paused for what seemed an eternity and Thika could barely stand the suspense. "I have agreed if you are interested."

Thika squealed with joy upon hearing the news from her father.

"Yes! Thank you father. I will make you proud, you will not regret it!"

"I am already proud of you Thika. Remember, you must listen to Baba Bautista's instructions at all times. Even if you do not agree. Do you understand?" Karanga raised one eyebrow toward her.

"Yes Baba."

Thika knew that her father would also have to convince her mother as well. Still, she appreciated his willingness to compromise and be open.

Karanga often returned home in the late hours of the night and arose before sunrise. He was a dedicated man to the cause of African liberation, and an even more loyal husband and father. Wambui watched him get older and more tired, and often felt a sense of guilt at her limited ability to take care of him. She was also very active in Alliance politics, and although she tried to fulfill the rest of her duties as a wife, she felt more strongly pulled to her duties as a political activist.

Wambui feared she was a bad example for her youngest daughter as well- one already resentful of gender roles since birth. Wambui had a cook, a maid and a gardener who completed household tasks, while she worked tirelessly for the Alliance.

Sex was also a duty she often neglected, although Karanga was never one to complain. She knew he could use more attention and affection. At Wambui's request, she and her husband had agreed several years earlier that Karanga would take another wife, a younger wife, after Thika had gone off to the university because Thika was so strongly opposed to polygamy that both parents thought it best to spare her until she was older and had moved out.

Wambui had been looking for the new wife for the past few months, and had settled on a young clerk who worked for the Alliance newspaper. She was from a good family, and was always modest in both appearance and attitude. Karanga had spoken to her only a few times in passing, and the plan was now in place to formally invite her into the marriage as his second wife.

Faza was beautiful and hard working, traits which pleased both Karanga and Wambui. She humbly accepted the proposal, and after a simple wedding, joined the household of the great General Mogi and Queen Mother Wambui. She was excited and afraid all at once; honored to now be a part of the "royal" family and afraid to fall short of the expectations that came with such a role. Faza was now intimate with Alliance politics, and she was destined to give birth to and mother some of the most respected and envied personalities in the region. Her new union put her, her future children, and her family at risk and came with it the ultimate responsibility of the health and welfare of the movement in general. But despite the obvious pressures of her new role, she was honored to be accepted in to the General's life. She had loved him in fairy tales as a child, admired him while studying Kenyan history in secondary school, and respected him as the object of many headlines in the Alliance newspaper where she was now employed.

Faza was groomed and instructed by Wambui to make the transition a smooth one, and she learned to value their relationship even more than that shared with her own mother. Wambui grew to love her as a daughter, and constantly instructed her on proper ways to please Karanga and the importance of being efficient and organized in a relationship.

"When he calls upon you, always be prepared. Be pleasant and helpful, never a burden or quarrelsome. He will be pleased with merely your company, he does not indulge in endless sex so do not expect or demand it. Give your honest opinion if asked about anything, even Alliance business or his relationship with members of the family. Your thoughts and suggestions will be valuable to him." Wambui gave a stream of suggestions.

Faza's blanket response to most instructions was, "Yes Maam."

Wambui would see the pleasure in Karanga's eyes when he spoke of Faza, and she knew that this was just the thing he needed to renew his spirit. Faza was a brand new love. She brought a freshness long ago lost between them. Wambui knew Karanga loved her as well, and she enjoyed all the privileges of being the first wife. Still she sometimes mourned the glory days of her and her husband's wild romance, and she envied Faza's obvious effect on her husband of twenty years.

The eventual news of Faza's pregnancy was celebrated throughout the Alliance, and soon to follow was Karanga's news of traveling to the United States. His announcement was not public; only his wives and top commanders knew of his plans. He had been summoned there to attend a Shepsu council meeting for PANA and would be away for one month. The trip would be a risky one, and in the event of his assassination, Wambui would become Commander-in-Chief of the Alliance. The news weighed heavily on Wambui as she called Shanzu and Thika home to visit their father before his departure. Karanga's top military aides had their instructions, and the move would begin in two weeks by way of China.

Wambui slid into the steaming water behind her husband, slowly messaging his temples as he lay safely wrapped in her smooth thighs. It had been rare that they had any quiet time alone, and she silently worried about the coming trip to the Americas.

He kissed her hands slowly and gently, as if not to break them. He too felt the weight of their coming separation and wished his older brother Masai were there to look after his family in his absence. Although they had not seen each other in many years, his brother was a silent supporter, both financially and in spirit, careful to not publicly support such an Alliance for fear of placing his own family in danger. It had taken Karanga twenty years to forgive his brother for leaving Africa and disengaging from African affairs. Karanga still found it difficult to reach out to his brother further.

"You received a letter from the States today." Wambui announced in a whisper as she washed his chest.

Karanga thought it odd to receive yet another correspondence from PANA. They were usually more careful regarding communication. "What is the news? Is there anything wrong?" he asked curiously.

"Your brother sends his greetings."

Everything stopped. Karanga was silent. He had not heard from Masai in a very long time.

She continued, "He would like to bring his wife and children to visit soon. They are considering moving back here to live."

She felt his body harden with anticipation. His thoughts were racing. She could feel his excitement.

"Move here? When?" Karanga asked.

"He did not reveal details, but wants to spend the summer here showing his family around. I assume you will be back from the U.S. by then? Maybe you could arrange to visit him while you are there."

"Yes. Maybe."

Chapter 7: Second Coming

Born in San Francisco in the early forties, Shaka was the second of four boys born to his soon to be single mother (his father later died in a riot in jail when Shaka was seven). His older brother "Tank" took over as man of the house and tried hard to help their mother raise three dynamic African-American boys.

By the time he was seventeen, Shaka had been in juvenile hall three times and was developing an anger problem strong enough to consume his entire life.

Tank, his mentor and confidant, had succumbed to the stress and powerlessness of being an impoverished African-American man by turning to drugs- a taste that many in the neighborhood had acquired and recommended.

The two younger boys had been placed in foster care after Shaka's mother, having been raped and beaten by her last boyfriend, was convicted of murdering her assailant, and sentenced to ten years in prison. Shaka was not allowed to visit her, because of his own criminal record, and vowed to avenge her wrongful incarceration. Every wrongful incarceration. His father had died at the hands of his country's "Just-Us" system and now his brothers and mother were all suffering a social and emotional death of sorts. He would become a fighter for freedom- a lawyer or judge or some other dictator of liberty. If he could survive parole and avoid prison, he'd be the peoples' Messiah: their salvation.

Shaka's aspirations were dampened by his fourth prison bit for a parole violation. It happened on his 21st birthday. Tank and his friends were taking him out on the town. It was not his first experience with alcohol. He first got "lit" when he was eleven years old and finished a bottle of Brandy his mother had left out after passing out drunk. But this time, he was with a group of older guys, men going to a club all dressed up and ready to dazzle some unsuspecting female.

On their way to the gig, a police car got behind them, ran the plates, and pulled them over. This was a daily occurrence for them all, not at all out of the ordinary. But it became a dangerous encounter because although not one of the men in the car was in possession of any illegal substance or weapon, the police had a way of "finding" or "discovering" items on your person or property, not previously there.

All the men were ushered off to jail after a bag of heroin was "found" in the trunk during the search. Shaka was on his last month of probation, but this violation meant another two years in prison. It was during this stretch that Shaka developed, shaped and focused his anger. He decided that in order to avoid set backs like this one, he would need to learn to anticipate problems and prevent them, instead of reacting to them as they came. Tank wrote him when he was close to being discharged.

Dear Shaka,

I hope this letter finds you in good spirits. I am looking forward to your release. It's been a long time, man. I have decided to move to South Carolina to get my life together and start over. Remember Mama's sister, Aunt Sadie? The one that laughs all the time even when nothing is really funny? Well, she invited us both to come live with her for a while. It would be good for us both I think, you know a change of pace. I hope you decide to come with me.

Love Tank

In South Carolina people seemed to smile more, the air was cleaner and motion was calmer. Everything was in slow motion, lazy and warm like a mother's womb. Shaka's uneasiness about his decision to come was quickly smothered by his Aunt Sadie's bear hugs and biscuits. He could barely breathe, his face sunk deep into her enormous breasts and enveloping heart.

Aunt Sadie had never had children and was delighted to have and care for two "favorite" nephews. Tank cleaned and sobered up and got a job at a local mechanics shop. He went to mechanic school at night, worked during the day, and made sure to help Auntie around the house and in the yard.

Shaka enrolled in the community college and later transferred to the university under a new program for ex-convicts. He studied political science and economics and minored in African studies. He was by far the most dangerous and dynamic brother on campus.

Shaka organized rallies and protests, lectures and study sessions about African history. He spoke convincingly to the African presence and importance in history, the present and our ultimate triumph in the future. He graduated with a double major and two bachelors degrees in Political Economics and African Studies. He later landed a job as a consultant to a large Black-owned computer software company, KEMTEL, while continuing his education in the Ph.D. program. He completed his thesis on the ancient African religions and their philosophies as the origin of all world spiritual beliefs.

Shaka had taken a two-year sabbatical from school after graduating to live in a nearby Yoruba community in South Carolina and learn the ways of his people's religion first hand. It was then that he first met Isabella. He learned through his studies that the practices between the ancient Kemetic

(Egypt), Yoruba (West Africa), and Santeria (Cuba), as well as Voodoo (Haiti and southern U.S.), and Condomble (Brazil) were almost identical in both belief and ritual. Pre-Columbian sea travel by early Africans and the transatlantic slave trade spread African beliefs and practices across the globe and may descendants of Africa were unaware of this fact. Many of the members of the Yoruba community he belonged to traveled to Brazil during the winter in honor of the annual celebration of Yemanya. It was during his first trip to Brazil that he would meet Isabella.

Isabella, or Bell as people called her, was Brazilian and a practicing member of the Condomble faith. She was an avid Pan-Africanist and political activist in Brazil. She and Shaka would stay awake sometimes the entire night talking politics, race relations, world economics and philosophy. They energized each other like two teens in their first romance. Each loved the other's fire and resolve.

Bell was a short, small-framed woman, no bigger than 110 pounds. She had light skin and deliberately wore her hair short. She and Shaka soon shared a physical relationship as well, and ached for one another whenever they were apart. They communicated regularly via computer, comparing notes on everything from the latest world headlines and upcoming Yoruba festivals to the monotony of everyday life.

"Mother has announced that she has figured out that I have a secret lover." Bell typed on her computer.

The internet was the way they communicated most often, as it was cheaper than speaking by phone. Bell was amused with her mother's excited discovery. She waved away a pestering fly as she laughed to herself. The humidity was high and the air motionless.

"Well, she is correct then. Did you confess?" Shaka typed, hunched over his laptop.

"No! She is certain it is a female lover! She says that no woman my age would be unmarried and childless unless she was lesbian." Bell chuckled as her fingers typed furiously over the keyboard.

It was cold in the Carolinas this time of year. Shaka grabbed a sweater from his bedpost and slipped it on. The naked woman in his bed barely stirred, apparently exhausted from the previous night's acrobatics. There was a steaming mug of coffee next to his screen that he sipped between sentences.

"I'll have to arrange a fitting disguise when I return then. Did you receive the package I sent you?"

"Yes. Thank you. The fabric is perfect. I'll show you my newest creation when you arrive."

The house smelled of sweet strawberries that Bell had brought home from the market. The fly launched from the fruit bowl, buzzed around the small room until it ended it's flight by resting on her computer screen. Bell brushed it away as she finished her email.

Shaka's position at KEMTEL was a lucrative one, so travel back and forth to Brazil was easy financially. His Portuguese was becoming near perfect – he had even developed the ability to joke, even flirt with Bell in his letters and emails. His Ph.D. in African Religious Theory allowed him to get an Assistant Professorship in the Black Studies Department at the University of South Carolina, and he had even started bringing some of his students along on his travels abroad. Graduate students and PhD candidates could travel abroad with him and complete theses on any number of topics: African philosophy, African spiritual thought or Culture and Religion. The trips fostered such robust academic results, that funding was made available to sustain a formal Study Abroad Program in his department.

His transcontinental love affair with Bell continued into its fifth year. It was an open relationship, with each taking local lovers from time to time. Neither ever married or had children. But they both were dedicated to the work, to the struggle and to Pan-Africanism, each aiding in its survival in their own small way.

Shaka imagined the thick, hot air of Brazil filling his lungs as he breathed deeply with eager anticipation of his return to Bell. He lay on his bed at home, staring at the ceiling, visiting her over and over in his mind. He could smell the salt of the ocean and feel the powdered mist on his face as he traveled the half-paved roads littered with people and trash. He could taste the spicy meat pie he would buy from a small boy on the corner and remember how the boy's feet looked hard and calloused; remnants of his impoverished life with no shoes. He would hear the thumping sounds of Brazilian music drumming its way into his chest and abdomen. People glistening with sweat in the summer sun, drinking beer and always smiling. Brazil was warm, lazy, sensual. It was welcoming and inviting. The palm trees waving with each cool breeze, calling him back again and again.

Chapter 8: Awakenings

Shaka's trip to Brazil to visit Bell seemed even more exciting, more intense than the last. Bell's voice was more urgent in her last letter, more serious. Shaka couldn't help but worry; she was usually so upbeat and optimistic. *Was she pregnant? Sick? Incarcerated?* This time, no students were invited to travel with him. He couldn't say what, but something about this trip was sure to change his life as he knew it.

Shaka had always been a pleasant site of a man, despite his forty years. He was six feet, four inches, a perfectly chiseled two hundred pounds, with strong hands, roaring voice and long sandy brown locks. Bell could feel his power at the airport even before she laid eyes on him. It was this power, this presence and wisdom beyond his years that assured her that it was time. What she was about to ask him would elevate their relationship and transcend all expectations of what their past union had been. He immediately beamed when he saw her, the bold, white hairs of his beard gently spreading as he erupted a slow, wide grin. His eyes danced with her vision – he had loved her and all that she represented for years: for what felt like his entire lifetime.

"Bem vindo de volta meu amor. Como vai?" Bell kissed Shaka lightly on both cheeks.

"Tudo e bom. Bom te ver Querida." Shaka stood back to take a good look at her.

"Your Portuguese is descent nowadays. You have been practicing, yes?"

"Yes, but it's difficult with so few people to practice with. Your English is pretty descent as well. We can practice more when we get to your house." Shaka's flirting had already begun.

Bell gave him a sly glance and winked.

"I don't need any practice, I've mastered what I need to know."

With that, she slipped her arm around his waist and motioned for him to walk with her.

As they walked to the bus stop, they quickly caught up on the latest happenings, family affairs and political atmosphere. Bell had started to take in homeless girls at her home and cared now for nine girls, three of whom had become mothers themselves. She spoke of them as if they were her own daughters. They lived off of Bell's humble salary as a seamstress and midwife, along with community donations from churches, schools, and PANA – the local underground political organization.

Shaka thought Bell a wonderful mother figure. He had quit KEMTEL, and was teaching full time. He also volunteered as a tutor at the local juvenile detention center for boys ages twelve to seventeen. He marveled at the energy and power of the young men and felt privileged to be involved in their potential enlightenment. He tutored math and reading, mostly basics openly, but once alone with the young African soldiers, also taught political science, African history and self-discipline. The boys soon trusted and admired him, and hungered for more knowledge.

Shaka was no doubt an excellent father figure, Bell thought. She had often wondered about the perfect family they may have had, had circumstances been different. But as it was, they were worlds apart and each playing an important role in their respective communities. Family to Bell, would be a distraction and a weakness and she thought it would hold each of them back from reaching their highest individual potentials. She had been pregnant for Shaka twice over the years, but had ended each pregnancy without his knowledge of their existence. Each time she was disappointed in herself for not taking stronger precautions.

They arrived at Bell's small house in the dusty underdeveloped countryside of Salvador, the bay side city in the state of Bahia in the northeast of the country. Shaka was surprised that the usual get down smell of home cooked food and the night of sweet, untamed passion with Bell was instead replaced with a house full of middle-aged militants gathered with what seemed to be an organized agenda. No giggling girls, no lingering aromas from the kitchen, no trips to heaven between Bell's thighs. Bell saw his eyes dim and his curiosity swell, and it was then that Shaka was first introduced to PANA.

"Everyone, this is Shaka. Shaka, these are my comrades." The room erupted into a jumbled collage of greetings.

"Ola Shaka."

"Oi brother."

"Welcome."

Bell introduced him to this brotha, that sista, all members of PANA – Pan African National Alliance. Shaka recognized a handful of this group from Candomble ceremonies he had attended in years prior. Bell was glowing with pride as she introduced Shaka to the group. The group, having obviously heard of him before, kindly nodded in recognition and warmly welcomed him.

Shaka knew of the group through Bell's intricate narrations of her involvement – he always wished something like this existed in the United States. The organization was international, with chapters in North and South America, Asia,

Australia, Europe and of course, Africa. It's
philosophy for Pan-African Nationalism – the belief
that people of joint African descent worldwide had a
common ancestry and common destiny.

That united ideologically was needed to
build, maintain and ensure the survival of the
African nation. PANA advocated for and believed
that Africans needed their own land base, as well as
a united political, social, religious and cultural
philosophy and that armed struggle would
eventually secure this fate for the people. In theory,
the governing body of PANA was made up of
twelve people worldwide, six male and six female.
Each was to be chosen for the people they struggled
for, with the aid of ancestral guidance. However,
the party had not secured chapters in the United
States up until that point, and at that time had only
ten Shepsu, an ancient African word meaning
"honored ancestor." Since this was the case,
committee members were chosen by those already
in the governing body.

Each Shepsu had to choose a surrogate as
well – someone who would replace them in case of
their untimely demise or incarceration. Bell had
been anointed Shepsu in Salvador after her
predecessor Santos, had been killed in a shoot out
with the Brazilian federal police. He was 53 years
old when he died, father of four, grandfather of two.
He had chosen her, without her knowledge, as his

surrogate, and at his funeral, she was approached by his wife and notified of her obligation. That was two years ago, and she had kept her role secret, as is required of all Shepsu – even from Shaka.

Shaka engaged in every philosophical and political conversation imaginable as he circulated the house. Upon news of his Bell's anointment, he felt a sudden rush of pride and admiration. He repeatedly commented on her strength and intelligence and spoke about how appropriate and timely their choice had been – as if Bell's anointment was recent.

Shaka basked in Bell's glory, honored to be an object of her much desired affection, and partied in her honor with the group until exhaustion set in and the once electric crowd fizzled out.

Still wearing the proud grin of the previous night, Shaka woke to the smell of home potatoes and Powfish, Bell's specialty, as well as the taste of her plump lips on his. She was delicious and smelled of peaches ripening in the sun. Her skin was glistening with sweat from the heavy Brazilian heat. He could feel her nipples hardening as she kissed and rubbed his bare chest and felt his nature swell and throb at her every touch. He had wanted to fill her up the night before, but was distracted by politics and revolution. Now as she panted and whispered love in his ear, she lifted her dress and straddled his now erect penis. He thanked God and the ancestors for such a beautifully spirited woman. She was light and easy to maneuver, as he slid in and out of her dripping center, her riding him like a professional jockey at the end of a smooth satisfying race. The chorus of moans was like an orchestra and her perfect breasts were like plums that cried red juice with his every bite.

The squeaking of the old bed soon joined the symphony of moans, and as always Bell came first. Shaka's penis jumped with every squeezing throb of her center, her head thrown back and her breasts frozen as if concentrated on every pulse. She melted around him, almost limp from the previous energy surge, but he knew how to redirect her.

He sat up with her still wrapped around him, and rubbed her head. He whispered how much he loved her. He kissed her softly – her head, mouth, neck. He breathed soft words of tenderness as he stood up and walked over to the kitchen table, the two of them still clutching each other in a dance. She loved it when he lifted her. He was strong and powerful, but gentle always.

They danced on the table, with each thrust more forceful than the last. He always looked her right in the eyes and silently talked to her with every motion. They moaned in turn and whispered to each other, his body trembling, flexing every muscle, until he released everything into her with such fire, that she cried long streams of tears and repeatedly confessed her love for him.

The food had been wrapped in foil and warming in the oven during the interlude. After taking a quick shower together, they inhaled breakfast like a pair of starved hyenas. Then Bell dropped the bomb.

"I've chosen you to be Shepsu, if you'll accept."

The sound of her spoon stirring her coffee was the lone echo in the room.

Shaka was silent for a long time. His mind raced with what responsibility he would have, the potential impact, or even impairment, he could have on the struggle. He had wanted this opportunity for what seemed his entire lifetime, but now briefly doubted his ability.

"How can you anoint someone, when you are so young?"

"Age is not an issue. Only what's in the heart that matters. I've been Shepsu for two years now, Shaka. I just never told you. I couldn't. You are more than qualified and you know it. I feel your energy and am certain that you will be an effective leader."

"What would be required of me?" Shaka was now gaining confidence.

"You would be responsible for securing members and soldiers in the United States, and for seeking and anointing the last Shepsu, a woman. Together you both will build a chapter of PANA, and along with the other Shepsu, help develop plans of action and political organization worldwide."

Oh is that all, Shaka thought.

"That is what I've wanted to do my entire life, Bell. I just didn't know how or where to start. Would I be trained or something before I return to the States?"

"This entire week is dedicated to your briefing and training. I'm scheduled to bring you to headquarters in an hour."

Shaka smiled "How did you know I'd accept?"

Bell walked over to Shaka and kissed him deeply, slowly. "You are too righteous a soul not to. There is one catch, however."

"What? I have to give my first born?" he asked clearly amused with himself.

"No. Shepsu are not allowed to be romantically involved with other Shepsu. It brings emotional distraction to the movement and jeopardizes its success." Bell was solemn, but firm.

They sat quietly together for a while. Her head rested on his chest, and she thought how she would miss this deep pounding heart that was now free to beat for someone new.

"I don't agree. The fuel of any revolution is love. It is what keeps up going despite impossible odds. It pushes us on in the face of potential harm. It persuades us to climb the insurmountable- to attempt the illogical."

"But you must admit that romantic feelings can also be a source of distraction. There may be times when a decision that is best for the group would be a strain on our individual relationship, thus creating a difficult conflict of interest."

"That is true if you look only from a material perspective. However, ours should be broader than that. Since our struggle is one for Africa and her descendants, our perspective is necessarily African. Thus, the notion of something being good for some, at the expense of others should be alien. In fact, it *is* alien. When we strive to take back our land, our freedom and our resources, we also strive to take back our cultural norms, our world view and our spiritual center."

Bell thought it certainly a compelling argument. She pondered his words in silence, wondering how the other Shepsu would regard them. Shaka was resolved to bring this topic up to the general body of Shepsu when the time was right. In the meantime, the intimate bond between he and Bell would need to be unseen.

Shaka's week was full of ideological discussion, guerilla combat and survival training, party briefings and political education. Each day started before sunrise and ended at midnight. Sleep was a luxury he rarely enjoyed. In fact, operating on limited sleep was part of the overall training. He studied the lives of Kwame Nkrumah, Franz Fanon, Assata Shakur and Nelson Mandela. He learned about the historic struggles for liberation in a variety of settings and times- Zumbi of Palmares in Brazil, Dessalines in Haiti and Yaa Asantewa of the Ashanti. His combat and survival training was under the watchful eye of Shepsu Antonio Bautista. Learning the art of hand to hand combat, securing food, shelter and hand-made weapons in the wilderness, as well as mastering field medicine and emergency preparedness filled his time with Bautista. He was oriented to several organizing techniques and strategies as well, and received training in how to work effectively with female comrades. The latter skill was essentially a lesson in respect, self awareness and humility.

Armed with ideological armor, Shaka returned to the States ready for warfare. He started by organizing political education study circles for students on campus, and secretly enrolling boys from his juvenile detention work. This expanded to a new enrollment program for ex-convicts to gain access to university registration, which is where he ultimately met Sarg. Virtually all of the brothers he encountered fresh out of jail were hungry for justice and jumped at the chance to be involved in a positive struggle.

Before long, Shaka had enrolled a formidable number of soldiers into PANA. With him as their captain, they were dangerous to the oppressive forces who had in the past directed their collective destiny.

The word had spread within the more conscious circles of the prison population like wildfire. Prisoners secretly pledged their lives to PANA and to the struggle, even before hitting the streets. It became illegal to be affiliated with PANA within prison walls for obvious reasons of endangerment to the white establishment, and guilty parties were punished by long time periods in isolation, or extension of already exaggerated prison sentences. The warden deemed it "gang affiliation" to justify the extreme consequences.

Chapter 9: Sister Love

Bluefields, Nicaragua

The ranch was an expanse of fruit trees, horse stables and combat training areas. Several horses ran freely through the groves and orchards, and the surrounding trees were home to local wildfire like exotic birds, monkeys, snakes. A large Cockatoo bird, as white as snow with a loud yellow crown sat on a low branch watching the re-union as if it had been a longstanding member of the family.

"Papa!"

All four girls ran recklessly toward their father, who dripping with sweat and dirt, had just come from the combat training camp in the countryside. Baba Antonio Bautista, weapons expert and tactics specialist, was the most infamous man within the PANA ranks. His eldest son, Simone was always by his side now that he had finished secondary school, with honors. He embraced all of the girls with a single swoop, and lifted them from the ground. Their legs dangled like wind chimes.

"My wonderful little ladies! How have things been in my absence?" He was exploding with pride and love at the touch of them.

"Fine!" they all harmonized, giggling with joy.

"And what of my big ladies?" he asked, surveying the ranch for signs of any of his wives.

He spotted Carla first, mother of the two youngest girls. She was a tall, light brown woman with wide hips, tree trunk legs and a round main of hair that she kept back in a single enormous powder puff most days. She was riding her favorite Stallion with Antonio's youngest son Pedro in her lap. Since the boys' birth two years before, his mother Esmeralda had been chronically ill and usually confined to the house. The other two wives had been caring for the boy and his mother since he was born.

Carla rode the massive animal over to where her husband stood. He swung himself up onto the horse's back behind his wife and embraced her waist with his strong arms. He wanted to kissed her slowly on the back of her neck, but knew better. She tolerated him for the ride to the house, careful not to show her displeasure to the mob of excited children. Carla was fond of Simone however, and eagerly inquired about how he had faired on this most recent trip.

"Have you been looking after your mothers, Pedro?" Antonio asked the toddler.

"Yes, Sir" the young boy replied in a squeaky raspy voice, his eyes as wide as the sky.

"Very well then. Where is Nazia?" Antonio asked Carla.

"She is in the house preparing food in honor of your return. She sent me to retrieve and wash you for supper."

Carla was terse as always. Together they slowly rode to the house. Two of the ranch dogs followed as they barked news of Antonio and Simone's return. A cloud of dust floated up behind the group as the sun swelled and spread over the horizon.

Nazia was Antonio's first wife and therefore in charge of the household. She was mother to Simone and Antonio's two eldest daughters. She wore her petite frame with the confidence of a lioness. Her skin was dark with a red hue and she wore her hair in two long braids on each side of her regal face. Nazia was comforting to those who knew her, but unsettling to those who didn't.

The task of being bathed was usually a time of extreme pleasure for Antonio. When the duty fell to Nazia, her gentle hands would send magical currents throughout his entire body. She was loving, generous and very thorough. But this was Carla. She deemed the task demeaning. A grown man should bathe himself. Thus, when he entered the room to find an empty tub beside which lay a towel and soap, he was not surprised. After his less than delightful self cleansing, Antonio floated into the kitchen, sweet with the smell of home cooked food and the even sweeter smell of Nazia.

The windows to the house were always open to encourage ventilation. Nazia grew several plants indoors, including an herb garden to use in preparing family meals. She was busy tending to children, stirring pots and doting over her nearly grown up son Simone. He was even more handsome than his father, she thought, rubbing one hand thru his hair while placing food in front of him with the other.

"He is growing into a fine young soldier, Mira." Antonio whispered in her ear as he lifted her from the kitchen floor. "And almost as good a shot as his mothers." he chuckled jokingly.

Nazia smiled, trying to hold back laughter with her hands. She was glad they had returned safely, something she would pray for with their every departure because Antonio was a very controversial figure in Nicaragua and was frequently made target by various political groups, both from within and outside of the country. The ranch had been under attack on several occasions, and with his frequent trips to Africa for PANA business, it became necessary for his wives to be skilled in weaponry and combat. Carla and Nazia had reputations handling guns, fit for lore and legend. They were both more accurate and aggressive than any man in the region. Antonio did not worry about them when he was away.

He did worry about Esmeralda however, his fragile young wife of only three years.

"How is Reli?" he Nazia asked apprehensively.

After her birth to Pedro, Esmeralda hadn't regained her strength.

He was now seating himself at the table to eat with the family. The plant vines lining the walls and ceiling gave the illusion of a large net, holding all in the room hostage.

"She is growing stronger everyday." Nazia announced proudly.

She felt like a mother to the young girl and was determined to nurse her back to health. Initially, Nazia blamed Antonio for the girl's illness. She and Carla had warned him against marrying one as young as she was- only 15 at the time. Nazia only agreed to the marriage after Antonio promised to not impregnate the young girl for at least three years. One year after the wedding, Esmeralda was already pregnant, and the birth was too much for such a juvenile body. She became violently ill during the birth, which ended in seizures and a partial stroke. She did not have the strength to hold

Pedro for five months, and eventually only after one year could she hold a spoon and feed herself.

Now, two years later, she was just able to stand alone, but not yet able to walk. Nazia had long since stopped blaming Antonio and now blamed herself. She should have taught the girl the ways to prevent, or even terminate pregnancy. She should have protected her or better yet empowered her. Instead, she abandoned her, and did not uphold the responsibility of a senior wife. She now worked around the clock, day in and day out, to rehabilitate Esmeralda.

Carla had nursed Pedro as an infant and assumed responsibility for his care, while Nazia cared for Reli. She fed her, read to her, taught her to stand again and to speak. She loved Esmeralda as a daughter, and Antonio knew the girl did not belong to him any longer. All matters of Reli had to go through Nazia first, a mountain Antonio neither had the will or strength to move.

After dinner, Antonio visited Nazia's room to update her on Alliance and PANA affairs, and to receive a report on household activities in his absence. The room was warm and dimly lit. Nazia was in the shower, the steam of the hot water filled her bedroom with mystery and secrets. Antonio sat on the floor of the washroom and talked to his wife from the outside of the shower door.

"I must travel again soon, but for the first time, I must leave Simone behind," Antonio called out.

"He will be angry. You know that Antonio."

"Yes, but it is necessary."

Nazia sighed. "I suppose it has its benefits. He can act as man of the house while you are away, it'll be good practice."

In truth, Nazia liked the idea of keeping her only son at home with her for once. She was also overcome with curiosity. Was this "necessary" because there was more danger than usual and he did not anticipate a safe return? She kept her wandering thoughts to herself, as she washed her body, then her hair.

"Yes, he *will* be man of the house while I am away." Antonio said, scratching his overgrown beard. He needed to shave.

"You know, he is taken with Karanga's youngest daughter." Nazia added.

She felt the need to speak more of their growing son. He was becoming a man, this was true. She wanted to hear his father's opinion of this young woman before he left them again.

"Thika?" Antonio said with a grin.

"Who else?" Nazia giggled.

" Yes, yes I did notice that. And she seems to be taken with him as well!"

Antonio liked Karanga's spirited daughter. She was a perfect match for their son.

"I've promised him I'd allow her a visit in the summer." he said with a smile.

"Then you must return safely, to keep your promise to him. The summer is nearly upon us."

"Yes, Mira. That I must."

Antonio smiled to himself.

Nazia exited the shower, as dark red and sleek as seaweed. He wrapped her in a towel, dried her hair and kissed her face.

"And my promise to you as well".

Antonio lifted Nazia and carried her over to the bed. He rubbed her body with oil, massaged her feet and brushed her hair. It was an unspoken rule on the ranch that upon return from any journey, Antonio always spent his first night with Nazia. She was his most comforting wife; she knew what to say to inspire him and motivate him to action. She could calm him, sooth his worries. She was the

Queen and master of the ranch, ultimately the caretaker of his other two wives and all of the children. Nazia did most of the cooking, cleaning and teaching. She alone made household decisions in Antonio's absence.

Carla was his fire, his wilder side. She could ride a horse and handle any weapon better than anyone in South America. She cried during her entire pregnancy with both girls, because Antonio forbid her from shooting while pregnant. She had killed several men during her lifetime, usually defending the honor of one of the local women. She was their spokesperson, their defender and advocate. Carla would not tolerate abuse of women, either physical or sexual, and her husband supported her in her life's mission.

Carla had first met Antonio at a cattle auction. She was selling the few remaining steers and a handful of heifers leftover from her father's ranch. The animals were under weight and she was obviously struggling financially to care for them. In a moment of pity, he offered to buy them for more than their worth and she had refused. He found out from a fellow rancher that her parents had both died in a gun fight defending their property when bandits attempted a cattle raid. Carla had successfully killed every bandit and was the sole survivor of the attack.

Carla quickly learned that male cattle drivers would not work for an unmarried woman. She had noticed Antonio at other auctions, as well as the local ammunition store and also knew he held a prominent position in the community. She would not however, take charity.

Antonio continued to display his concern in various ways. He would have animal feed delivered to her ranch. She would send it back. He would send Simone to assist her with ranch chores. She paid the boy despite his objections. She later sent Antonio a letter.

Senior Bautista,

Your generosity has not gone unnoticed. However, I find it dishonorable that you would offer such assistance without the consent of your wife. Surely she must know of your actions, if not your intentions. I am not even sure of your intentions. I must ask you to cease in your efforts concerning my welfare until a proper communication is sent by way of your wife.

Sincerely, Senora Carla Vega

Nazia thought Antonio's proposition a humorous one. She liked the stern tone of Carla's letter. She liked that she was being given deference by this self assured woman. She also liked the idea of helping her, even in this unusual way. Carla was a brave woman. Antonio proposed that they invite Carla into their household; into their marriage even, as a second wife.

Antonio was sure that this was the only way Carla would consider joining their family. It would not be seen as charity and Carla would be gaining a new family. She could either sell her parents' ranch or hire hands to run it, which ever she preferred. Nazia would have help at the Bautista ranch and with the children. Nazia weighed the deal in her head and after several months, finally agreed.

"Well, that is truly a generous offer Senora Bautista." Carla sipped her tiny cup of coffee, all the while holding Nazia's gaze in her own.

The two woman sat in Nazia's kitchen. Carla had agreed to meet Nazia there for lunch, after a formal invitation was sent by way of Simone.

"But tell me, is it your idea or your husband's?" Carla asked with obvious suspicion.

"My husband's." Nazia knew what question would follow.

"Why would you consent? Why share your husband with a total stranger? Do I seem to be in urgent need of a savior?" Carla was clearly insulted.

Nazia remained calm and soothing.

"It makes business sense. After all Senora, marriages are merely business contracts. I need assistance at my home, as do you. It is beneficial to us both to consolidate households. His wants are secondary." Nazia could see that Carla was visibly pleased.

"If I agree, the deal will not come with sexual duties as other marriages do." This was a statement, not a question. "Physical intimacy must be optional as far as I am concerned."

Nazia thoughtfully considered the statement.

"Understood and agreed. Since the agreement would be between us two women, Antonio would have to comply with any terms we determine. However, I must insist that any lovers taken on your part be discrete and not bring any shame to our family."

Nazia stared at Carla with a concrete poker face.

"Of course." Carla sat back in her chair, a slow grin sweeping across her face.

The first few years of marriage to Carla were exhausting for both Antonio and Nazia. Although she was very helpful in a multitude of ways, Carla was an ever active women's advocate in the community and never far from excitement.

Carla had ridden the horse to near exhaustion. As she raced up to the ranch gates, she announced her arrival with a shout known to all inside to signal trouble. She motion to Simone to close the gates behind her. Antonio and Nazia were already armed in response to her warning.

"What is it?" Antonio was short, stern.

"I killed a man. He was trying to rape Louisa. His brother is not far behind." Carla spoke in an urgent tone.

She dismounted the large animal and went to reload her rifle. Antonio looked at Simone, then Nazia. Carla was always in some kind of "situation".

"Come." He motioned for Simone to accompany him.

They were gone for a little less than an hour and then returned. Carla's pursuer was not with them. Antonio dismounted his horse and walked into the house. He embraced Carla and kissed her on the forehead.

"Aim for the leg next time, sweetheart."

He then turned and walked into the kitchen.

The entire episode was secretly exciting and amused him. That night after dinner, he made voracious love to Carla, his fearless, soft, sensual wife. It was one of the few times she had allowed and reciprocated his affections.

When Esmeralda fell ill, Carla too blamed Antonio. She was disgusted by him and had since rejected him from her bed. Carla's hatred for him grew so strong that she appeared at Reli's bedside with a rifle whenever Antonio came to inquire about her. His visits soon dwindled to almost nothing and he would simply get updates from Nazia. Carla adopted Pedro as her own, taking care to bring him to visit Reli several times a day. She knew that her son was Reli's motivation to get better. Pedro was her strength.

The night of Antonio's return this night however, was full with Nazia. Far from the bitterness he received constantly from Carla or the grief and guilt he felt for Esmeralda, his times with Nazia were always rejuvenating. She healed him and comforted him. She encouraged and forgave him. Her body wrapped around his for endless hours of wet passion. Soft, shallow pants echoed thru the night, only to be muted by the begging moans of desperate lovers.

Nazia awoke the next morning content and satisfied. She was still full of Antonio from their night together. She kissed his back as he lay snoring in the morning sun's glow.

"Remember your promise Antonio." She whispered to him.

Nazia and Carla had reminded Antonio that part of Reli's recovery would be her reconnection with him. Now nearly 19, she needed to be made to feel like a whole woman. Nazia cared for her, Carla gave her the satisfaction of helping with her son. Antonio had not shown any affection to her since Pedro's birth three years prior, partly because of his guilt and partly because of the wrath of the other wives. There was the occasional shallow kiss on the head, but nothing more. His guilt was overwhelming and the women knew it would be hard for him, but they insisted. His affection was the missing piece to the puzzle of her slow recovery.

Many nights would pass before he would get the courage to visit Reli's room. She lay on the bed reading, and when he pushed the squeaking door open, her gaze slowly drifted up toward his face. He never said a word, just smiled a warm smile and sat next to her on the towering mattress. He cupped her face in his hands, and kissed her mouth slowly, now tasting the salt water that flowed from her perfect doll's eyes.

"I missed you Reli." he whispered. "I'm so sorry."

He began to cry. Esmeralda gently wiped his face with her hand. She had not fully regained all control of her extremities, but she concentrated with all her might, and tried to comfort her husband. She tried, with much difficulty to remove her dress, even rejecting his attempts to help her. She fell to the floor once, but determined, stood up again. Once fully nude, she took two steps toward Antonio. They were her first steps since Pedro's birth. He met her in the middle of the room, and they both cried uncontrollably. Antonio helped her back to the bed where he made very slow, careful love to her that night.

Although everyone agreed that Esmeralda's recovery seemed to quicken after that night, Carla and Nazia made it clear to Antonio that he had served his purpose and was to never touch the girl again.

Chapter 10: Queen's Horses

Oakland, California

"Baby, I need to tell you something." Wiz tried out to herself.

No. That's not it. Try again.

"Sweetheart, what would you say if..."

Definitely not. He'll see that coming a mile away.

Wisdom practiced endlessly, but could not settle on a way to tell her husband of the coming events in their home. He'd surely say "No" and accuse her of being completely insane. Surely, he should be able appreciate the magnitude of this situation. Of course, he would be able to see the importance of aiding in such an effort, after all they had met in a political organization in college- one whose aim was also to assist in freeing African people. But she was sure that convincing him to leave with the children, leaving her behind to host a meeting in their house, full of strangers- that would be an altogether different undertaking.

Masai returned with the children after a full day of soccer. All three children stood in the kitchen, panting like puppies, with the smell to match, and rattled on about who made what goal, the score and the overall excitement of their Saturday.

Wisdom kissed them all and sent each upstairs to bathe and prepare to eat. She had been cooking and rehearsing her lines all afternoon in anticipation of her family's return. Masai embraced his wife and inhaled her very essence as deeply as he could. He loved her, and was himself curious to see how she would take the news of a trip to Kenya. He hadn't been back in years and was considering moving back.

Wiz and Masai had discussed the possibility of moving there before, and once he had finished his degree in engineering, the conversations became more frequent, the planning more detailed. He had been searching for business opportunities there, and had just received an offer as Project Coordinator for a new jet engine system being developed through the military. He was excited and couldn't wait to share the news with Wisdom.

To investigate the opportunity more thoroughly, Masai decided it was necessary to travel to Kenya and spend the summer there touring the facility, looking for homes, perhaps even visiting his brother Karanga. The offer was a very generous one, and he felt that travel to the continent as soon as possible was crucial.

He had practiced all afternoon on the soccer field what he would say to his wife, but now with her in his arms, he drew a blank. Why was this so difficult? She had already agreed to move there someday, right? He knew she loved her career here, as well as the close relationship she shared with her parents and brothers. But, she'd have a new family in Kenya; his family. Surely, she could continue her medical career there. The children would complete the school year this week and then have a break over the summer. Perfect timing!

His cluttered thoughts were interrupted by an intense heat building between his legs. Wisdom's hand had made its way inside his pants and encouraged his middle to swell and throb with pleasure. She kissed his chest and guided him onto the kitchen floor.

Never mind, he thought to himself. *I'll tell her later.*

He tried to hold back the screams of delight as his wife rode him gently up to the clouds and back. The journey would end sweetly as his warm stream traveled through her body furiously, leaving his dark, tall body limp and serene. She kissed him again slowly and sent him upstairs to shower and prepare to eat as well.

Alright, she thought. *I'll wait and tell him later.*

The morning brought bright sunshine and birdsong gliding through the window like a sweet fragrance. Wisdom's head lay on her husband's chest and the symphony of his heartbeat and the rising and falling of his chest with every breath would soothe her in and out of cozy slumber. The children could be heard arguing in the distance, just distant enough for them both to ignore. Masai rubbed her bare back and kissed her head.

"I got an offer in Kenya, Wiz. I want us to go there this summer to check it out."

She lay perfectly still in bed, her thoughts racing.

"That's wonderful Baba! When do we leave?"

He was surprised by her enthusiasm.

"The kids will be out of school in a week, but realistically it'll take two to three weeks to get all of the travel arrangements done."

She pondered on what that would mean for the upcoming meeting scheduled to take place in exactly two weeks. She had to be there, her family had to be absent.

Masai continued. "I've sent Karanga word of our planned arrival. I'm waiting to hear back from him."

Together Wiz and Masai mapped out all the details, dates of travel and duration of time in Kenya. Wisdom would have to stay behind and work a few weeks before joining her family in Nairobi. She had several responsibilities at the hospital that would need her full attention before being absent for such a long interval. Masai agreed, but made her promise not to travel alone. East Africa had become quite the boiling pot, and he was concerned for her safe arrival. Perhaps her father or one of her brothers could accompany her.

Wisdom promised, and with what seemed to be a concrete plan in order, found no reason to worry her husband with the news of an international political assembly scheduled to take place in their home while he was away.

During breakfast, the plans were shared with the children, who expressed a fleeting moment of disapproval. They would miss their friends and cousins. What if no one remembered them in Kenya? Once reminded of the friends they made on the last trip, and that they would be free to write and visit old friends here in the States, the objections became less forceful. The initial reservations soon transformed into excitement at the thought of embarking upon such an adventure.

After the two weeks had passed, plans were solidified, and farewells recited, Wisdom stood at the window of the airport waving goodbye to her family as they soared back home- eager to form new relationships, new ideals and new destinies.

Chapter 11: Blue Strangers

Oakland, California

Shaka would be the first of twelve to arrive that night. Sarg had coached Wiz on each person's personality and how to best interact with everybody individually. The revolution was not without egos, envy and lust among other things, he had reminded her.

Shaka, he explained, was the easiest of all.

The PANA Shepsu arrived one-by-one, via bus, taxi, bikes, trains. Some wore rags, others fine attire, but all wore the resolve of a determined people. The elders had been summoned together before, to analyze the goings on of things, give advice and direction, prophecy. They were the chosen in their respective communities, to represent each voice. But this time was different. Shaka knew that the entire direction and success of the movement- this quest for freedom that had engulfed and captured the soul and minds of his people- depended on the outcome of this one gathering. His mind ached with questions and possibilities.

As he arranged chairs and poured water he pondered how this of all nights, was not a time for phone taps, snitches, provocateurs, infiltrators, police raids or beat downs. Oakland had been chosen as the meeting place. After all, the fame of the Panthers was born and ultimately laid to rest here. The energy of the freedom movement made transition here- from black beats to saggin' black dockers, afros to dreadlocks, power handshakes to "pounds" and strong embrace.

Shaka had arrived the night before in disguise as was always necessary. He had gotten a job as a cook on a cruise ship from Cuba and had later road a bus from Miami. He was complete with ragged, dirty, urine laced clothing, occasionally mumbling a word or giggle to himself. He then dragged himself over to a nearby gas station where he patiently stood and chanted "spare change" to passersby. It was nearly four hours before Sarg would drop a dollar into the greasy blistered hands with an address on the back and disappeared into the neighborhood traffic. It had been five years since Shaka had seen Sarg. He had missed him like a son, but masked his emotion. He looked forward to seeing and talking to him later that evening. He walked what seemed to be miles before approaching the address of the house he had been instructed to travel.

A single light shone toward the rear of the house. Shaka walked up the back stairs and opened the unlocked door to the porch. He removed his shoes, bowed to the altar facing him and thanked the creator and the ancestors for a safe journey. As he knelt on both knees, eyes closed and heart open, he suddenly could smell sweet jasmine and amber oil. The hair on the back of his neck rose, and he lost his breath for an instant. His eyes opened to the sight of a curvy, caramel toned woman. Wisdom was sturdy and solid, yet welcoming. She floated toward him, fluid like ripples of water.

"Greetings Wisdom." Shaka kept his back to her for a few moments, then turned to finally meet her. "Thank you for your hospitality."

"Welcome Brother Shaka. How were your travels?" She extended her hand to shake his.

"Tiring, but good." He took her hand in his and kissed it. His lips were warm on the back of Wiz's hand.

"There is fresh fruit and plenty of cold water in the kitchen. Clean towels, soap and shampoo are on the top shelf in the washroom. Please sleep in the second room on the left. The Sarg has extra clothes there for you. Leave the clothes you have on where you are standing and I'll wash them in the morning. Sleep well."

That first night at Wisdom's home was not a restful one for Shaka. Braided dreams of his intriguing hostess, the agenda of the long-awaited gathering, and stabbing worries of security leaks, made slumber a mere aspiration far from reach. His lingering thoughts of Bell, in anticipation of her arrival made his mind race out of control, to the point of exhaustion. Sarg had developed into an extraordinary soldier and military leader, and Shaka knew that with him at the head of security, the lives of everyone involved were in the most capable of hands. He also knew however, that all prior Shepsu meetings had been plagued with death and violence, as counterintelligence tactics of the enemy eventually seeped into the cracks of their efforts.

The sweet smell of jasmine oil lured his mind back to thoughts of Wisdom. He had heard every detail of her life from Sarg, who took every opportunity to deflect any praise for his actions over to his older sister. Shaka felt her power with every fond memory. He had chosen her for his surrogate and intended to inform her this morning. He had already confided this fact to both Bendi and Jahmilah, his immediate superior, and his recent recruit. Both women were skeptical of his choice; someone he had yet to meet. But Shaka was determined that this was someone destined to be Shepsu one day.

The next morning, a soft knock at the door aroused Shaka to attention.

"Yes, please enter."

"Good morning. Antonio and Chebuke have arrived, and there has been a security meeting scheduled to take place in the basement in one hour. Food will be provided at this meeting. Can I get you anything?"

Wisdom was very to the point and neutral in speech. She had been informed by Sarg that although Shaka was an extraordinary man, his one weakness was women- beautiful, powerful women- and that all her interactions with him should be uninviting.

He should have absolutely no problem with me then, Wisdom thought. Never had she been accused of being neither beautiful nor powerful. She smiled to herself at how ridiculous it all was, and appreciated her brother's generous words and pretentious concern. Nonetheless, she followed his instruction.

"No, I have everything I need." Shaka said with a mesmerizing smile. "Sarg has trained you well." he added proudly. He paused, then continued. "And vice versa I might add."

Wisdom's palms began to sweat and her face felt hot. *What the hell is wrong with me?*, she wondered.

Shaka walked closer to where she was standing at the door. He was shirtless when he emerged from the bed, with loose fitting cotton bottoms draping his lower body.

"By the way, what exactly has he told you about our organization, about this meeting?"

He looked into her eyes until she looked away.

"Enough." Wiz said confidently, trying to disguise her nervousness.

"Enough to be Shepsu?" Shaka asked toyingly. He enjoyed making women feel uneasy.

Her discomfort sent surges of energy through his body.

"You don't need more Shepsu." *Bastard.* Why was he flirting so openly and playing this obnoxious game? She was married, for Pete's sake!

"Every Shepsu needs a surrogate; someone to take his or her place in the unfortunate event of their demise. I have chosen you as my surrogate. That is, if you accept."

His invitation hung in the air like a cloud.

"Why not Sarg?" Wiz asked, now interested.

"He already has a large responsibility within PANA, one that he does better than anything and anyone else."

"What would I have to do?"

She's in, he thought. "Is that an acceptance?" his voice rang with victory.

"I'd have to discuss it with my husband and he'll be away for three months."

Shaka was now frowning.

"I need an answer by nightfall. Only then will any responsibilities be revealed to you."

He knew she'd accept. She only needed time to wear the decision for awhile, break it in. The first round of Shepsu meetings would start at noon.

Wisdom turned to leave the room, again charged with task of joining the revolution, a challenge she welcomed with apprehension.

Now, as Shaka paced circles around the room, anticipating Wiz's return and the arrival of the elders, he aspired to make theirs as pleasant an arrival as his had been. Each was coming from a distant place, every region of Africa, the Caribbean, South America, Europe, Australia and Asia. All African people. Leaders. Warriors. Careful steps had been taken to ensure that each had traveled as unrecognized as he had. Lives were endangered by entering the land of "Babylon." Especially to plot her demise.

It was common knowledge that a meeting of such high ranking officials in PANA would be known by the European and American intelligence agencies, and thus by Interpol. Ever since the liberation and unification of East Africa, an aggressive campaign to dismantle PANA had been underway by European nations and their allies. African raw materials and natural resources were too valuable to be in the hands of her native people, and strategies were developed to undermine the legitimacy of the movement. Interpol had designated the group a terrorist organization.

PANA counter-intelligence had learned that Interpol's plan was to disrupt the meeting and assassinate as many PANA senior officials as possible. Interpol's base was to operate out of the local police department, in cooperation with the FBI. However, PANA had other plans. They would mount a preemptive strike and take out all communications abilities of their enemy just prior to the Shepsu meeting, thus ensuring successful completion of the meeting and it's mission.

The explosion could be felt for a ten-mile radius and the mushroom of black smoke in the sky was the signal to the assembled Shepsu that the meeting could proceed as planned. They had exactly four days to organize a massive offensive attack worldwide. Precautions were taken to ensure that the station was free of any people, to avoid any casualties. Orders were specific that no loss of life was desired, merely destruction of property.

Sarg motioned to Bird and Shug to flank the entrance to the Central Police Station downtown, now a heap of rubble and smoke. The blast was designed to leave no functioning equipment, and now the trio would investigate to confirm that outcome. They entered the wounded structure dressed in gas masks and toting heat sensing devices attached to the high powered rifles each man had is his possession. Anything that was salvageable, was carried back to the Shepsu meeting.

Chebuke, PANA's communication specialist, had scrambled the city's communication systems minutes before the attack, and the enemy's lack of communication and absent central ground attack made the sabotage of PANA's efforts virtually impossible. Once secured, the station was tapped for future information gathering and defense. Sarg and the others then crept back into the night without a trace, later joining the rest of the PANA members.

When Bendi first arrived at the house, Wisdom found it difficult to not stare. Her striking light hazel eyes, short dark blonde hair with grey and white streaks, and copper skin contrasted like flickering stars across a midnight sky. It was as if she had been spray-painted with bronze glaze. She had the hands of a man- thick, scarred, strong, with the grip of a python.

"Why you in dis free business, daughter?" Bendi was holding both of Wiz's hands in hers. "Bruddah Shaka say dis you camp eh?"

"Yes Maam." Wiz could tell that the elder woman was fond of her already. "I want to help in whatever way I can. Please, come and sit." Wiz motioned for Bendi to sit next to her.

"Solid girl." Bendi's crinkled face smoothed with her smile. "Where you child?"

"My children are with there father in Kenya. I will join them there when the meeting is over." She handed the old woman a hot cup of tea.

"Dat deadly mob der. Good business." Wiz strained to understand Bendi's pidgin, but by following her tone and body language, knew the Bendi was complimenting the work the Alliance was doing in East Africa.

Bendi Papuan, the eldest living Shepsu, was an aboriginal Australian and farmer. She, her husband and their four adult children ran a large farm in south-central Australia, also home to PANA's Institute of Agriculture and Horticulture.

The institute was home to hundreds of students, agricultural scientists and traditional healers.

Munjaree, Australia

The vast Australian countryside was brown and dry, but the institute was a well of life and greenery, a solitary spring in the center of the desert. It accepted scientists from other struggling nations for training and exchange of knowledge. All were engaged in the pursuit of obtaining sustainable forms of both energy and agriculture. She was a quiet woman, with a soft, round face; slowed by age and of little words.

Bendi had the sole authority to call Shepsu meetings, and had done so rarely- only when circumstances required. In the circle of Shepsu, she and Nahsi were the eldest, had the most history in PANA and worked closely as advisors to the general body.

This meeting, she had called after an attack of PANA headquarters in Ethiopia. The East African Alliance was building a monstrous momentum, and the latest recruit Somalia was scheduled to join by month's end. A large congress was underway, full of Alliance and PANA diplomats eager to greet the Somali delegation and secure the newest addition to this political giant. The attack had killed nine crucial government officials, two news reporters and forty three civilians.

All knew it was an attempt by hostile Euro-American forces to destabilize the region and slow the growing surge of unity and independence in Africa. PANA would now move from the building, organizing, education and political stage, to their military, national defense stage. The summoned Shepsu would meet to orchestrate a worldwide insurrection- one that could possibly mean either the long-awaited prosperity or total annihilation of African people everywhere.

Bendi reminded Wisdom of Wiz's grandmother "Wise". During the four-day meeting, Bendi found time to help Wiz cook food, lend parenting advice and even share secrets of several medicinal herbs. The elder woman, knowing that Wisdom had been chosen as Shaka's surrogate and the eventual hardening that comes with politics and revolution, was determined to share with her younger counterpart the virtues of maintaining some semblance of femininity. She liked Wisdom; she was not yet tainted and scarred by war, and Bendi wanted her to stay that way.

Chapter 12: Winter Breezes

Oakland, California

Wiz received each Shepsu into her home with a deliberate caution. Each was from a different corner of the globe, with different customs and norms, and she was careful to be respectful of each. One by one they arrived, some in the young hours of the dusk, some at dawn and yet still others in the deep darkness of night.

Jamilah Akbar was a devoted wife and mother of four daughters and the latest appointed Shepsu. She had been raised Muslim and spent her entire childhood in Mosque number 26 on 106th street in Harlem. She arrived in a full length garment with her hair completely covered.

"As-salam alaykum sister." Jamilah cooed to Wiz and kissed her on her cheek.

"Wa alaykum salam." Wiz was comfortable with Jamilah in her current pregnant state, something Wiz was keenly in tuned with.

Ripe with child, Jamilah had a tall, slender frame, with a crane's neck and delicate hands. Her slim profile was punctuated with a large, round belly which held her fifth child.

Theresa Cisneros had been anointed Shepsu one year before giving birth to her, now 11 year old son Diego. She was an elementary school teacher in Cuba, and volunteered in the fields picking strawberries on her days off. She was a warm and friendly woman with a wide smile and even wider backside.

"Bienvenido Senora Cisneros." Wiz was unusually formal in her greeting.

"Mucho gusto Mira. Please, call me Theresa." She handed Wiz a bouquet of flowers.

Theresa's face was striking and angular, made all the more noticeable by her completely bald head.

Theresa's arrival was followed shortly by Chebuke Kamathi who was based in Brixton, London. Chebuke was the communications commander in PANA. He was a computer wizard who could master even the most complicated machinery and stood 6 feet 7 inches tall. He wore small framed glasses and a short afro, with his towering body matched by his massive, muscular frame. He was also the stand-in father to Diego, Theresa's son, whose biological father had been killed at the hands of his uncles when he was nearly a year old. The sexual tension between Teresa and Chebuke was evident, and Wiz wondered if there might be some secret history or maybe even ongoing relationship.

Hai Nan arrived from Phnom Penh, Cambodia. It was the first time Wiz had ever seen someone from Asia with such a dark complexion. The night Nan arrived, they talked for hours about the African heritage of much of Asia and the various groups there that fight to keep that history known and alive. An accomplished professor in Economics at Phnom Penh University, she was also a consultant in international business and trade for several corporations in Cambodia. Her most recent publications included *"Imperial Economics- The Race to Under Develop the World"* and *"My Fathers Word: A Linguistic History of SouthEast Asia and Her African Roots."*

Kua Ovambo was a bioscientist at Genetec Laboratories in Namibe, Angola. She was a short, round woman with a sizable gap in her two front teeth. She wore a multitude of braids all combined in a hive at the crown of her head. Her husband Zumbi was the BioDefense Coordinator for PANA, but remained in Angola to continue working on development of a vaccine for Linz Virus, the newest in biological warfare.

Nahsi Kedah was an "untouchable" of Southwest India. He was deep bronze in color, had long locks that danced behind his knees with every step, and was a devout Shiite Muslim. Married, with two adult sons, he ran a fishing and boating business off the coast of India, and spent the remainder of his time politically organizing the darker peoples of his subcontinent. He greeted Wiz with a long bow followed by a strong embrace. He was, by far the most affectionate of the Shepsu so far.

Pierre LaRoque was the Chief of Health and Medical Research in PANA, and was based in Haiti. His greeting was similarly affectionate, with a slow soft kiss on each side of her face.

"Bonsoir Madame."

Pierre's eyes were set very deep inside his skull giving him the unsettling appearance of a zombie, Wiz thought.

"Bienvenue Monsieur."

Wiz showed him to his sleeping quarters, and then later the clinic downstairs. Pierre was very complimentary at Wisdom's level of preparedness.

After his wife had died in childbirth, Pierre vowed to spend his life to helping others and he became an honored doctor and researcher within the impoverished Haitian community. He had managed to raise his daughter Monique, now sixteen, alone.

Antonio Bautista and Isabella arrived approximately 2 hours apart. They had traveled part of their journey together since they were both coming from South America. Finally, most of the

Shepsu had arrived and Wiz patiently awaited the arrival of the final Shepsu. Meanwhile, she continued her role as hostess and tried to make each guest as comfortable and prepared as possible.

When Karanga arrived, Wisdom was shocked into silence at the sight of her brother-in-law. She and Masai had been told all these years that he was a politician in the Kenyan government, but not this! Masai had discussed with her several times wild rumors that his brother was some terrorist renegade. They had even laughed at the ridiculous sound of it all. Now, it was becoming clear. His identity as leader of the Alliance was one he kept hidden from his brother. Maybe it was only kept from Wisdom herself? Was it for security reasons? To protect his brother or his family from the dangers of this political jungle or protect his precious revolution from his weak, westernized brother? She disapproved of the secrecy and was curious of his intentions.

Karanga was equally shocked at the sight of his brother's wife. All Shepsu meeting places were kept secret and secure and he had no prior knowledge that he was traveling to his brother's home. How was she involved in PANA? And where was Masai? She had obviously kept her political involvements secret from her husband, a behavior he found unacceptable for an African wife.

He disapproved of the secrecy and also questioned her intentions.

They greeted each other with a cold disgust, each too self-absorbed to notice the inherent awkwardness of their re-union.

"What are *you* doing here?" they said at the same time.

After a short pause, Karanga spoke first.

"I am Shepsu. *I belong* here." He said firmly, as if Wiz did not belong.

"Well, I was chosen to be surrogate and asked to host the meeting." Wiz shot back. "My brother is a security officer in PANA." Her voice had a resolutely "I -do-belong-here" tone.

"Does Masai know your involvement?"

"Not yet."

"Typical! Where is he?" Karanga was now shouting.

"He's in Kenya, with you I thought. And typical of what?"

"Never mind, it is not important. You are to pack up all of your things and promptly join my brother in Kenya. You are not allowed to be surrogate because I have chosen him for one, and Shepsu cannot be in relationships with one another."

Karanga spoke as if Wisdom was his daughter and he was giving her some simple cooking instruction. He had now calmed his voice, but spoke very deliberately, very directed.

"No, no." Wisdom sang in the inclining tone one speaks to a baby when about to touch something forbidden. "It is you who have to choose someone else, because I've already accepted my role." She pointed her finger into his chest with every syllable.

"No!" He was now shouting again. "You must rescind your acceptance! In my brother's absence I am responsible for you, and I insist!".

He insists? Now that was funny!

"Karanga," Wiz began as if she was speaking to a four year-old. "I am responsible for me. And I say, choose another!"

She marched away, insane with anger, and a trail of black smoke streaming behind her head, now engulfed in flames of rage. *Responsible for me, my ass!* She continued to mumble to herself behind the privacy of the bedroom door.

Bird looked on and chuckled to himself at the sight of her screaming at such a powerful man. Karanga was clearly not commonly spoken to in such a manner. Bird knew he had his work cut out for him- trying to protect a volcano from the rain was definitely going to require focus, and skill.

Downstairs, Comrade Bautista walked slowly as he inspected the arsenal. The young sergeant had done well. Wisdom's basement was fully stocked with weapons, ammunition, bulletproof vests, night vision goggles and surveillance as well as communication equipment. Sarg's soldiers were equally as impressive, as they stood at full attention until the commander from South America acknowledged them and ordered them to stand at ease. His first lieutenants, Shug and Bird had jumped at this chance to protect and serve. The others were a mix of men from various backgrounds; active and ex gang members, born again military veterans, soldiers from the Nation of Islam and a small wing of the North American PANA military. Even Dee's two bodyguards had volunteered. Naim Akbar, Jahmilah's husband, had enlisted with the sole purpose of protecting his wife and unborn child. All had been in training for several months, specifically for this assignment. All knew the magnitude of the task, and that it might be their last.

In the kitchen, the whisper of steam rolled off of the lake of hot tea that filled the mug. Theresa stood at the counter, looking into the deep chamomile lake as if to get a signal or sign. She did not hear Chebuke enter the kitchen, but could feel the temperature rise to a cozy warm the closer he got. He walked up behind her, pressing his firm middle against her as he breathed into the hair on the back of her head and held her hands to the countertop. Her heart pounded. She wanted to turn around and devour him, but remained still, facing forward. She was wet and aroused. As was he.

"Where is our son?" he whispered heavily down her neck.

"With my mother." she said. Her spine tingled with sweet anticipation.

"Does he have his ticket to London?" His passion was not yet at full attention but it was getting there.

"Yes. He has his instructions. He will be gone when I return."

She reached one hand back and stroked his neck. Her nipples puckered as her blouse brushed over them.

"I'll take good care of him. And you." He moved his face around to her ear and kissed it. Slow. Deep.

"I know you will. Be careful, love."

And then as gracefully as he had come, he was gone.

Chebuke had assembled a central surveillance center, with full audio and visual sensors surrounding the perimeter of the house, as well as direct interception of all internal local and federal law enforcement communications. Sarg had mapped out all escape routes from the house, and earlier had privately placed Bird in charge of ensuring the personal safety of Wisdom.

Soldiers were on guard around the clock, both inside Wiz's house, around the immediate perimeter, snipers in positions in all four directions and remote security at points within a five and ten mile radius.

Shaka, one of the three newest Shepsu since the last international meeting, had corresponded with both Chebuke and Bautista on several occasions beforehand, but this was their first personal encounter. He was proud that Sarg had represented them both so well.

The men did a complete inventory of all equipment, checked that everything was functioning properly and that all Shepsu had personal and separate escape plans. Bautista, Shaka and Chebuke then all ran various drills with the team to test their readiness. Several potential scenarios were represented in the drills, and upon successful completion of each, the resolve of the group swelled like an ocean wave about to crash onto shore.

The security meeting ended with a finale speech by Shaka.

"I commend you all in your bravery. You each answered this call to protect the future of the people."

Shaka paced before the group of men, his nostrils flaring with each word.

"The enemy we are fighting, the entire European Imperial Complex, including Interpol as it's enforcing body, is a viscous one. It is an intelligent and calculating one. One without conscious or morals, without regret or mercy. We all must be willing to live and die defending our women, our children, ourselves and each other. We must the protect the idea of collective freedom."

There was no cheering. No applause. Merely heavy silence. Explosive contemplation.

Wisdom and Bendi had been in and out of the basement with food and water for the congregation of men. The energy of the room and the sight of the dark army ignited something in Wisdom that had been laid to rest after the birth of her first child. Now resurrected, it boiled to the top of her head, and she felt like a stallion just before the gates open for the race. She suppressed her impulse to smile and hug the familiar faces in the room; her brother, Shug and Bird. She was restless and anxious to get started. It was this moment that she decided to accept Shaka's prior invitation. She would swallow this news until nightfall. Bendi stood quietly toward the back of the room and motioned to Bautista. He directed everyone's attention to the small woman and informed them of her status.

"Mama Bendi is the eldest Shepsu. She is the greatest of us all. She is our strength and our conscious. Give her your full attention and devotion." Antonio spoke with great emotion and pride.

As the eldest living Shepsu, she was the leader of the movement and all decisions had to ultimately be given her approval. The men towered over her as she parted the sea of them with her determined walk. In her soft voice, she spoke with strength and authority.

"All Shepsu come now. Please dress dem good for de meetin'. When de sun jumps up, de booliman want come, so be careful eh? Thank you all foya strent."

She faced them and offered a slow nod for appreciation and respect.

"Baba Bautista, get dem men ready. We begin in two hours."

"Yes, Mama Bendi, of course." he replied, offering a bow to the small giant, his fist across his chest and eyes gazed to the ground.

She placed one hand on his head for a moment and then turned and left the room.

Wisdom, initially dazed and not knowing what she was to do, was finally escorted out on the wings of Bendi's tall spirit, her feet seemingly never touching the ground. This woman of many years, quiet voice and small body, had the presence of the universe, vast and infinite. Wisdom loved the power of that moment. The room full of men was subdued in Bendi's presence, ready to follow her every instruction.

Wisdom gathered the Shepsu and escorted each one to the basement to receive their vests and weapons. She and Bendi had been busy earlier preparing food and were therefore the last to be fitted. Wisdom felt like the Terminator in all of the garb, and twenty pounds heavier. How was she supposed to function in a full suit of armor? She was excluded from the Shepsu meeting, but forbidden from leaving the house or using the phone due to safety concerns, as well as to not distract the attention of the security team. She decided to pass the time writing to Masai and the children. She missed them and looked forward to joining them in Kenya in a month.

Baba,

I hope you and the children have arrived safely in Kenya. I miss you all terribly and look forward to joining you soon. The distance between us will shorten with each coming day. I love you.

Wisdom

Unknown to Wisdom, Bird watched her every move, as were his instructions from Sarg. Through surveillance cameras, windows, audiotapes and personal encounters, there was never a moment when Wisdom was out of Bird's sight. He watched her laugh to herself when writing to her family, sing into the cucumber-microphone while preparing meals for Shepsu and pretending to be Aretha Franklin. She danced to reggae music, painted wonderful paintings of her children and read poetry to her husband out loud even though he wasn't there.

He saw her try to be brave and polished in front of the Shepsu, and then later cry herself to sleep at night. He was sometimes angry that she was being made to endure this much, but more often proud of how she was struggling to be strong and reliable. He always felt uncomfortable when it was time for her to use the toilet or shower. *Surely, she deserved some privacy*, he thought. But he knew that at any moment, harm could befall her, and he was the only barrier to that happening. He was determined to protect her always, which meant sometimes invading her privacy. He never spoke of it to anyone, especially to Sarg. Bird was growing to love Wisdom with his entire essence. He breathed her in as deeply as he could whenever in her presence. He would die for her. More importantly, he would live for her.

Chapter 13: Birth Song

Bendi and Nahsi sat at the far ends of the table, and together they facilitated the Shepsu meeting. They were the matriarch and patriarch of PANA and oversaw the international movement toward liberation. Bendi's stout build and wild blonde mane contrasted starkly with Nahsi's lean frame, which was covered with thick cascading locks on every side. Nahsi called the PANA meeting to order.

"Welcome."

Nahsi's lazy eyes and slow drawal were warm and comforting.

"Tis been long time since we last meet." He was nodding and acknowledging every member with his knowing stare. "Please brethren, give us word of the security first and then the medical report."

Chebuke, Karanga, Bautista and Shaka sat at the four corners of the long rectangular table. On the left side sat Teresa, Pierre La Roque and Jamilah Akbar. To the right side of the table, between Karanga and Shaka, sat Hai-Nan, Kua and Isabella.

Baba Bautista gave his report first. He reviewed each Shepsu's escape plan, in the event premature evacuation became necessary, gave a complete weapons inventory and security team update. Earlier he had ensured that each Shepsu was armed and vested, and had secured emergency exits from the basement. This was followed by Pierre's medical report. He was introduced to PANA after a five year friendship with Kua, whom he met at an international medical conference of Infectious Diseases and Bioterrorism. Since then, he had opened several PANA satellite clinics in Haiti and throughout the Caribbean.

Upon arrival to Wisdom's home, Pierre had done an inventory of all medical supplies, as well as gave Wisdom a detailed crash course in guerilla medicine, in case such skills were needed during the gathering. Now, during the meeting he gave an inventory of supplies and reported that all involved parties, including members of the security team, had been supplied with emergency morphine, personalized emergency medical kits and a small vial of "liberty"- a potent chemical substance aimed at ending one's life if he or she desired to escape torture or confession.

Satisfied with the two reports, Nahsi continued along the agenda. Since the last Shepsu meeting seven years prior, three new Shepsu had been welcomed into the family and three lost to the struggle. A moment of silence and prayer were offered for those who had given their lives for the revolution.

"Give love to the newest of us. Sister Isabella de Santos Cardoso of Brasil."

The group all responded with one single united clap.

"Brother KaShaka Williams of the United States."

Another single group clap followed.

"And Sister Jamilah Akbar, also of the United States." Each were enthusiastically welcomed into the ranks.

Each Shepsu announced his or her surrogates and Bendi took care to record each, along with the surrogate's level of training thus far. It was decided that Wisdom Masters, Shaka's newly appointed surrogate would need to begin training immediately after the meeting, and that Karanga would need to work quickly in replacing his surrogate. Karanga remained silent.

"Today we will spend discussing our offensive objectives." Nahsi continued. "The remainder of our time here in the next days will be spent broken up into smaller groups for planning, and we will end the meeting with a final plan of action."

Nahsi looked around into the eyes of each person as he spoke. He then nodded to Bendi in acknowledgement of her coming comments.

Bendi smiled a reflective grin prior to speaking. She slowly sipped from her cup of tea, then inhaled deeply before releasing a deliberate, tranquil breath.

"The tower in Ettiopia been attack. Dem say the attack was by de Europe booliman. The World Bank give money to dem boys. We hafta strike back swif. Baba Karanga will lead dis attack from the base in Kenya with de Alliance help. Dis big business, we in PANA must be organize and ready. De target is de enemy mother station in Spain, and two more substations in Australia and Germany. The attacks must be at same time."

She then sat back with her hands folded on the table. "What questions we have?"

The room exploded with questions, comments and utter confusion. The energy was electric, and only after numerous attempts did Nahsi finally regain order.

"Order yourselves people. Get your sense back now." Nahsi's hands were raised out over the group.

Slowly, the group molded a plan of action and by nightfall the initial dull blade of insecurities sharpened into a dangerous sword of determination. The next two days would be a series of smaller committee meetings, followed by the closing general Shepsu gathering.

There were six committees, each headed by two Shepsu. Baba Bautista and Isabella were head of the Military division. Communications was headed by Chebuke and Jamilah. Pierre and Kua ran the division of Health and Science, Shaka and Teresa were heads of Education, and Karanga and Hai-Nan were responsible for the Governmental branch of PANA. Nahsi and Bendi spearheaded the Agricultural wing, and each Shepsu pair met separately, around the clock until all objectives were finalized.

Wisdom stayed very busy during this time. Food for this group, supplies for another. Ensuring all had clean towels, soap, and deodorant. Jamilah had a specific diet, as did Nahsi and Hai-Nan. Shaka required candles for prayer, Isabella required music to think. Pierre had to have a glass of French wine with every meal. Was he for real? The security team needed food and water around the clock.

Wisdom began to look forward to her water runs. It was the only time she was allowed outdoors. The sun, the wind and the trees were like old friends she enjoyed seeing again. Bird escorted her to every soldier in need of water or supplies. She figured he must have one of the lower ranks to be regulated to assist the "water girl". It was unfair, she thought. He was clearly dedicated and sweet, and she liked him. Those old guys must be jealous of his youth. Bird was principled and had the chiseled body of a stone sculpture. He had no caveman thoughts or behaviors like Karanga. No, "I want to eat you like a cookie" look on his face like Shaka.

Responsible for me my ass! She fought to control the smoke now trying to escape from under her hair. *Calm down Wiz*, she thought, *and enjoy the fresh air and even fresher company.*

Bird and Wiz had brief conversations during water rounds. She learned that he had joined PANA against his wife's will, and that she had left him because he chose another "gang" over her and their family. His sadness about his terminated relationship was obvious, but it lifted when he spoke of his children. His wife agreed to never keep him from them, and that was his comfort throughout the entire breakup. He said he'd hope to find a woman just as dedicated to the struggle as Wisdom someday.

"Initially I feared helping and even now have some guilt for excluding my husband in my decision." Wiz glowed when she spoke of her brother Sarg and their exciting childhood together.

"Sarg talked me into it. Everyone has doubts at some point. At first I was even skeptical of Sarg's friendship with you." Wiz looked down in embarrassment. "The 'gang banger' was all I could think of when he would tell me about you. I thought it was not a good friendship for him. But now I know better." She looked up and smiled at Bird with those last words.

Wiz shared her birth stories, Bird shared war stories. She spoke of Masai and how sensible he had turned out despite his backward Kenyan upbringing. She wanted to trash Karanga with her words, but resisted. Bird knew it, and was amused.

Each soldier had a small break, one at a time, at mealtimes, and Wisdom always stayed to eat with her brother Sarg and Bird when it was their turn. For the others, she would bring them food, then promptly leave.

In the midst of an afternoon lunch date with Wisdom, Sarg confided that he had assigned Bird to be her personal guard.

"I had to Wiz, things are going to heat up soon. Promise me you will follow any instructions Bird gives you." Sarg gave his sister Wisdom a long, serious gaze.

"Ok, I promise. Don't be so doom and gloom." Wiz said with a nervous laugh.

Sarg reviewed Wiz's escape route with her and confirmed she knew how to use her firearm. He also gave her a small pocketknife and showed her how to use it.

"You got your passport and documents?" his voice now quivering with emotion.

"Yes. What about you?" she said in her mothering tone.

"I'm good, sis." He hugged her with more force and feeling that ever before, feeling the stiffness of her bulletproof vest under her clothing, then kissed her on her forehead.

Wisdom could sense that the meeting was soon to be over, even though it wasn't scheduled to conclude until the next day. That evening, she walked through her house, and stepped passed each memory it held along the way. She looked into the children's rooms and heard their laughter linger in the walls. She walked to the basement and said her goodbyes to the colossal Harriet on the wall, holding the soul of every baby born and soldier who died from within that very room. She turned off the light and walked upstairs to the kitchen, where the dirty dishes sat, waiting for her company. She ran some hot water, cleared the table and placed any salvageable food in the refrigerator.

In silence she stood over the sink reviewing in her mind the day's events, when the lights began to flicker. It was the silent alarm that Chebuke had installed to go off whenever there was a breech in security. It meant immediate evacuation.

Wisdom's heart began to beat harder and faster. Her hands trembled. She left the water running and quickly fell to the floor. She crawled to the hallway and frantically tried to remember her escape route. The bathroom window! That's it! She did not see or hear any other Shepsu in the house and wondered if she was alone. The crawl down the hallway would be roughly ten yards. She peeked around the corner, and seeing a clear passage, she went for it. She made it to the bathroom door, reached up to turn the knob, but it was locked. Locked! What idiot was on the toilet at a time like this? *Okay, Wiz- plan B. Plan B.* There was no fucking plan B! *Calm down- think.*

She removed the knife from her pocket that Sarg had given to her earlier that day. She tried to pick the lock, but no success. Then she jammed the knife into the knob hinge and the door swung open. Shit! There was blood on the floor! She slammed the door shut, and sat on the hallway floor horrified. *No way am I going that route!* She crawled down the hall further to the laundry room, the flickering lights of the house a constant reminder of her eminent danger. She entered to a flurry of gunfire, the silenced fire sounded like flying darts, and she quickly returned to the bathroom in one single leap. She opened the door, gun cocked and poised and entered, locking the door behind her.

There she saw Karanga. He was sitting on the toilet, pants around his ankles with both his tongue and his penis completely severed and placed in each of his hands. His eyes, feet and ears were removed as well, and the entire bathroom floor was an ocean of his blood. She could feel the vomit boiling up from her stomach, into her throat and finally onto the floor. The window was open and she slowly walked over to it, her sorrow for Karanga growing with every step. He had died a painful death, one without dignity or beauty. But it did have meaning- a fact that she would communicate to Masai. The doorknob to the bathroom turned slowly, awakening Wisdom from her somber thoughts. She quickly climbed up to the window ledge, when the door came crashing down and a shower of bullets unleashed their fury onto her body. The bullets stung like wild honeybees, then carried her three stories down to the cold, damp ground below.

Darkness. Wisdom could hear faint sounds in the distance, but could only see darkness. She couldn't feel herself breathing. She could not move any part of her body. Then, all sound stopped. Her heartbeat became harder to hear, and her body grew as cold as a frozen lake.

Chapter 14: Falling Bricks

Ngong Hills, Nairobi, Kenya

Wambui was as tall and deep as Masai had remembered. She welcomed him and the children home as if they had only been away for a few days.

"The prodigal son returns eh?" Wambui was flashing her entire set of teeth through her immense smile. She approached Masai with open arms and wrapped him in an inescapable bear hug.

"Wambui I see you still have your exquisite gift of exaggeration." Masai was also smiling.

"Auntie!" Masai and Wisdom's children seemingly tackled Wambui, smothering her with an array of hugs and kisses.

The day was filled with food, laughter and fond remembrances of older times. They looked at old photographs of Masai and Karanga when they were boys, and Masai told long, exaggerated tails of their childhood adventures together. Shanzu and Thika adored the children and spent most of the time entertaining them and sneaking bits of candy into their pockets when no one was looking. They braided Iyana's long, thick hair and watched the boys chase chickens in the yard.

Wambui assigned a guard and driver to Masai whenever he left the grounds, and provided a list of good housing opportunities as well. *He is skinnier than his brother*, Wambui thought as she embraced him every morning before his departure. By the end of that first week, Masai felt pampered by all the attention. His meals were prepared like clockwork, his clothes washed and pressed. Wambui shaved him daily, and he often returned to the General's palace in sheer delight at the thought of what he may encounter next. The children were always waiting to share the days excitement with him, and his nieces; the picture of respect and righteousness. He missed Wisdom desperately however, and kept a journal every night in which he'd record his daily agenda and his deepest thoughts and feelings to her.

Two weeks had passed and he was bursting with excitement as the day of his wife's arrival drew nigh. He wanted to tell her that he had made his decision and wanted to accept the job in Kenya. He had found a wonderful home for their family in the countryside, near a mission hospital where Wiz could work.

After taking the children on a visit to the city, Masai returned one day to find a wooden box on his bed. Inside, it contained a letter from his brother Karanga, placed there no doubt by Wambui. Karanga had traveled abroad on business prior to Masai's arrival, and was due to return around the time Wisdom was due in from the states.

Dear brother.

If is had become necessary to deliver this to you, I fear that my return to my family has become an impossibility. Wambui was only to reveal it to you in the event of my not returning and I trust that our common blood runs deep enough to afford my faith in you. I know that the fate of our struggle as a family, as a people, as a Nation is in good hands-your Hands.

Your Ndugu, Karanga

Masai placed the letter on the bed. He stared blankly into the bed, holding his breath with paused heart and heavy chest. *Me?* he wondered. Masai knew it was tradition that when a man died prematurely, the responsibilities of his household was adopted by his brother. Karanga had two wives, two adult daughters and was expecting another child. His "household" consisted of the entire East African region, which he had been head of for several years. Being accepted as leader of an entire region of Africa would also be an impossible mountain to climb. Masai had only one wife, who surely would object to now being one of three. He had three young children, whom he also assumed would reject the unusual arrangement.

Karanga is alive, he thought. He hoped. *He must be.*

The letter went on to give very detailed instructions, contacts, codes and deadlines. Wambui and Karanga's second-in-command, Lt. Mugabe had also been given instructions to aid and assist the new leader of the Alliance, and make the transition as smooth as possible. Shanzu and Thika were also made aware of the recent happenings and both wore their grief for their father in bold patterns of anger and mistrust toward Masai. Wambui remained very poised and always kept business in the forefront of her interaction with him. Alliance business. Household business.

"It is time that you interacted with Faza." Wambui spoke solemnly, never raising her eyes to his. "She is far along in her pregnancy and continues to act as an outsider in her new family. She must feel isolated."

Masai was silent. The multitude of responsibilities showered him in despair.

Wambui did what she could to train Faza, but her responsibilities in the government kept her away often. Meanwhile, Thika resented her father's new young wife.

"We are the same age, she and I. It is shameful really." Thika growled in disgust. "She does not belong here. What does she bring of any value?"

"What does anyone bring to a new family? New ideas. New energy." Shanzu replied.

Shanzu liked the young girl, and thought her respectful and kind.

"Companionship is a basic need of all. Father is a powerful man, and mother very important and powerful as well. Faza could have filled the role of companion to both of them in time. Now, she will do for Uncle Masai what she would have done for father."

Shanzu also liked that Faza had finished school and actually had intelligent thoughts and opinions on most things. Shanzu kept such conversations to a minimum however, out of loyalty to her sister and respect for Thika's disdain for polygamy. With Karanga gone, Faza became virtually invisible in the home and felt isolated, often times overwhelmed with sadness. Wambui was very aware of this despite her seeming indifference.

"Women are like chameleons my dear child. We can change with the environment. You will now embrace your new marriage to Karanga's brother, Masai. Do not let sadness hold your heart captive." Wambui struggled to mask her own nagging despair.

Wambui communicated with all involved and planned Karanga's burial ceremony. She arranged the public military ceremony of Masai's inauguration as Alliance leader, as well as plan the two separate wedding ceremonies necessary for him to finalize his marriage to both Wambui and Faza. The whirlwind of plans, meetings and expectations left Masai intoxicated and exhausted. He just wanted Wisdom to hurry and return, which was somehow delayed. Three weeks had come and gone with no sign of her. He had received few letters from her since arriving in Kenya, and she did not mention arriving late, so he assumed all plans were continuing on schedule.

Dearest Masai,

Things are wrapping up on this end and soon I will be reunited with you and the children. How are they? I'm sure being spoiled by auntie Wambui no doubt. I hope everything is proceeding as planned on that end. I can't wait to see you and touch you. My nights are cold without you.

Wisdom

But, plans were not continuing on schedule. In fact, all previous plans had been de-railed and Masai felt a wave of anxiety as he received news of the schedule change. He later received the notification from PANA explaining that Wiz was missing.

Comrade Masai,

We regret to inform you that your brother Karanga has been murdered and your wife Wisdom's current location is not apparent at this time. During the Shepsu meeting at your home in the United States, the gathering was interrupted by hostile forces necessitating immediate evacuation.

The news sent Masai into a virtual panic. *Why didn't Karanga inform me he was traveling to my home? And Wisdom?* Wisdom had never kept anything from him before. Certainly not something so big. According to the letter, she was last seen alive under the protection of PANA soldiers, but her exact location was still unknown.

General, you are advised to stay in Kenya and await further details. Being a Shepsu surrogate, as well as the wife of the esteemed General, please trust that it is our utter duty and intention to return her to you as soon as is possible.

Forward Ever

Meanwhile, his instructions were to lead an offensive attack against a Dutch ship off the coast of Ethiopia carrying weapons to local mercenaries.

Masai sat remembering his and Karanga's childhood. His grief began to well up like a hot spring, and he sat quietly wiping tears from his lifeless face.

Masai remembered the pet monkey they shared as boys escape from its cage and terrorize the village children. He held his belly and smiled remembering how it had ached, as they both laughed uncontrollably. He remembered with pride how they both tackled their father to the ground to interrupt the beating he would inflict on their mother. The family farm, with Jackie the dog and Jack the cat, was home to goats, cows, chickens, five boys and the constant onslaught of visiting neighbors and helping hands. He looked out of the window and saw young Karanga's tear filled eyes as he waved goodbye to Masai en route to boarding school. That had been their last year together as boys. Now they were together as men.

Wambui insisted that all burial and wedding arrangements be complete prior to launching any attack. Masai agreed to bury his brother's memory, but was ashamed at his discomfort with the marriages. It was *custom*, and had been his entire life. Somehow his stay in America had changed his world view and altered his loyalties. He needed to talk to Wisdom first obviously. He needed her approval. He needed to proclaim his undying love for her, to her, and explain away the circumstances.

Wambui assured him that the choice was neither his, nor Wisdom's to make. History and custom had made it for him. The future of Africans around the globe depended on the success of the

Alliance and PANA, and that success rode largely on the trust in and loyalty to its leader. No one would support him if he left his brother's family unspoken for, and rejected his cultural traditions. His public acceptance of Wambui and Faza was just as instrumental as his public acceptance of the Alliance presidency. The two were interconnected. There was no time to await the arrival of Wisdom, she would be completely debriefed of the entire situation upon her arrival. And so it had been decided. And so it was.

Chapter 15: Motivations

Los Padres, Southern California

There was a single bed in the room; no other furniture and no windows. The hardwood floor was covered by a soft, red Persian carpet in its center, with a black dog lying on it comfortably asleep. No, it was a brown bear. Yes, definitely a bear. The bear sat up when it realized that something was moving on the bed, and then the bear spoke.

"Try not to move baby. You're pretty beat up." Wiz was stunned.

The bear placed his strong paw on her forehead, the heat of his breath against her face felt somehow familiar.

I'm either dead or in a lockdown facility for crazy people, Wisdom thought as she marveled at the speaking bear, and repeatedly blinked her eyes to gain better focus.

The bear's face slowly melted into the soft face of her wonderfully sweet guardian. It was no bear at all, but Bird, her lovely keeper, companion and protector. Her entire body hurt.

"You're lucky to be alive. That was a long fall." Wiz could hear the concern in Bird's voice.

Wiz opened her mouth as if to speak, but no words formed on her tongue.

Bird continued. "It took a while to drag you out of there. We took heavy fire. Alot of people didn't make it." He paused and gazed down at his hands. "We're at Dee's safe house. Nothing to do now but get you stronger and ready to travel."

Dee kept a separate safe house for any women trying to escape abusive pimps, husbands or both. The house was stocked with food and clothes, and her bodyguards had been instructed that anyone from the "gathering" at Wisdom's place in need of laying low for a while was welcome to take advantage of its confidential location. Most of the bullets hit Wisdom in the chest, in her bulletproof vest, but the force of the blast was enough to render her unconscious. She reached down toward her leg, suddenly aware of the throbbing she had been experiencing there.

"You were shot in the leg. I removed the two bullets. Hope the bandages aren't too tight."

She looked down at her bandaged leg. She had on a nightgown and thick socks, no underclothes. The vest was gone, the mud she was sure she had tasted the night before, was also gone from her mouth.

"How long have I been asleep?" Wiz finally managed to squeak out a few words.

She sat up quickly, which made her head pound in agony. She slowly laid back down.

"Two days." Bird was happy Wisdom had finally come around.

"I bathed you and dressed you in clean clothes. I tried to clean out your mouth as best I could. I hope that was okay."

My mouth?

Wisdom was embarrassed.

And *Bird saw me naked? How had I managed to go to the bathroom? Had he cleaned that up also?* She was horrified at the thought and tried to put it out of her mind. What about her brother?

"Where is Sarg?" she asked with fear in her raspy voice.

"Safe. He has an assignment to finish. He'll be alright."

"Karanga is dead. I saw him in the bathroom." She continued the sentence in her mind without a sound. She then started to cry.

She had treated him so poorly, and was now ashamed of her previous behavior. Her husband's brother had died away from his family and friends, on the toilet, in the house of his crazy, uncultured sister-in-law without dignity or ceremony.

Bird hated to see Wisdom cry. He wasn't exactly sure what to do or say.

"Yes, I know. But we made sure we got a lot more of them." Bird tried to force a smile.

Great, Bird. That'll make a girl feel better, he thought to himself.

He was instantly frustrated with his response and tried again.

"Wisdom, we have to keep moving. No time to get stuck in the past. I have instructions to take you to Kenya."

Wisdom felt relieved. If only she could be reunited with Masai, everything would be better. She wanted to tell him about everything that had happened in his absence.

"But first, we must spend a small while in South America." Bird said reluctantly.

"South America?! Why?" Wiz was crying again.

This is just fucking great, Bird thought. *Here we go with the tears again.*

"Those are my instructions, Wiz. Please don't make it hard for me." Bird was now pleading.

"Hard for you? Alright, I'll try not to make it too hard for *you!*" Wiz was trying not to get upset. It made her head hurt more.

Bird stood up, turned toward the door and walked out. He stood out in the hallway to give her some time to think and space to breath. He needed time and space too. He wanted to hold her in his arms, kiss her and promise to make it all easy for her. But he knew it wouldn't be easy. It was only going to get harder. She was vulnerable at that moment; away from her husband, her children, her brother. He loved her and didn't want her to fall victim to either of their weakened states and regret it later. He would have to keep a respectful distance while trying to shelter her from her loneliness and rescue her from her fears.

Dee's safe house was in a discrete location in California's central valley. Women from all walks of life were there: street wise prostitutes, sheltered housewives and wise old grandmothers. All of the women shared in household chores, security and lending of free advice. Wiz sat at the kitchen table while across from her Dee explained the fake ID's she had obtained for the coming trip.

"Never thought I'd see you of all people in any trouble girl." Dee was wiping Wiz's left eye, still puffy from the fall and prone to spontaneous tears.

Dee was visibly shaken by Wiz's current situation.

"Me neither." Wiz managed a half smile until her face started to hurt.

"These ID's will get you where ever you need to go. Study them so you seem natural answering to a new name. Now you do everything that young man tells you understand? Take care of yourself Wisdom." Dee reached across the table and held Wisdom's hand.

"I will Dee. Promise." Wiz stared into Dee's eyes and squeezed her hand.

Dee's eyes welled up. She stood up, bent over Wiz and hugged her and then turned to leave the room.

Wisdom and Bird both had passports and documents with alternate identities, as was PANA's protocol with all of its members. To elude any authorities potentially on their trail, it was necessary to travel an indirect route out of the country.

Together, they stayed with Dee and Ashanti at the women's palace, spent a few nights at various gang homes and even one night with some of Shug's family. Within one week, they boarded an airplane for Peru, where they then traveled by jeep to Nicaragua. The entire journey took nine days total, and when they finally arrived at the Nicaraguan border, PANA soldiers escorted them to the ranch of Baba Antonio Bautista.

Bluefields, Nicaragua

The ranch was vast and reached as far as the eyes could see. Bird and Wisdom were greeted at the gate by Carla and Simone. Apparently, Antonio had not returned home yet from the happenings in the States. The two were mounted atop a pair of the most beautiful horses Wisdom had ever seen. They also possessed two other horses without riders, presumably for Bird and Wisdom. Wisdom's feet hurt, she was dirty and stinky, and she melted into the animal's back, barely able to sit up straight or keep her eyes open.

The surrounding trees lured her gaze with tempting low hanging fruit, almost within her reach. But, her arms were anchored to the horse, unable to be coerced upward.

Simone and Bird did all the talking and sleeping arrangements, as well as security provisions for the night were made. Bird and

Wisdom were assigned to share a room during their stay there, a room with its own bathroom, a separate entrance from the outside, and a single bed.

Carla gave Wisdom clean towels and shampoo, and instructed her on how to get to the kitchen when they were done cleaning up. She collected the dirty clothes they had traveled in, and left each standing in the shared bedroom wrapped in towels. Wisdom would bathe first, then Bird. Together they made their way to the kitchen where they would meet Nazia, Esmeralda and all of the children. Wiz would also see Thika.

Thika? What is my niece doing here? Wiz wondered.

It had been arranged by her father prior to his departure for the Shepsu meeting, that Thika was to come and learn combat training from Baba Bautista and spend the entire summer in Nicaragua. Apparently, since arriving two weeks before, the puppy love she shared with Bautista's son Simone, had grown into a big dog marriage proposal and engagement. Simone had begun Thika's combat training in his father's absence, and his three mothers had begun grooming and training her as his future wife.

Thika hugged Wisdom intensely and gave her cheerful updates about Masai and the children.

"They are beautiful Wisdom, all of them. And smart! They keep everyone at the palace busy and youthful." Thika was very upbeat and happy and wondering out loud what Wisdom was doing in Nicaragua. "What are you doing here? Masai is expecting you in Kenya by now I'm sure."

She doesn't know, Wiz thought in horror. *She doesn't know about what happened at the meeting.*

Thika clearly didn't know about her father. Wisdom thought it best to keep it that way for now.

Better she find out from her mother or her future husband.

She kissed Thika, and with an equal amount of enthusiasm asked of her wedding plans, school and the like.

"Just a short detour, nothing more. I'll arrive in Kenya before you know it." Wisdom was doing well disguising her dishonesty. "I had no idea you were even old enough to date, let alone marry." Wisdom nudged her niece playfully.

"I'm old enough to do alot of things Auntie." Thika said in her most mischievous voice.

The entire family ate and basked in the glory of their togetherness until nightfall. Then all of the women retired to their rooms, even Thika now had her own room in the house, and Bird and Wisdom retired to theirs.

For the first week, Wisdom slept in the bed, and Bird slept on the floor. After listening to Bird flop around on the hard floor for several nights, eventually Wisdom allowed him to move to the bed, but she would be under and him over the blankets. It was also necessary for their heads to be at opposite ends of the bed. During the days, he would watch on as Carla would train both Wisdom and Thika in the arts of shooting and archery. Simone would teach martial arts, hand-to-hand combat and the science of creating explosives. Each had to learn to ride a horse, drive combat vehicles and fly an airplane with expert precision and skill. Carla sat on the wooden fence post watching Thika and Wisdom during target practice. Pedro was focused intently on suckling at her breast, as he sat on her lap pulling her nipple between his teeth as he attempted to watch the women as well.

"Again!" Carla called to the two initiates. "Like this," she continued, removing Pedro from her now sore nipple and tucking her breast inside her shirt.

She hopped off of the fence and grabbed her own crossbow. She again demonstrated the proper form and force. She released the arrow into the air, slicing through it and directly onto the center of the target. Wisdom and Thika studied her technique and began again.

All meals were prepared by Nazia and Esmeralda. Matters of politics and combat were often topics of conversation over the dinner table. Wisdom thought the entire arrangement a bit peculiar. Carla was clearly a strong woman- the strongest, most passionate woman Wisdom had ever met. Nazia was strong as well, but in a different way. She was solid, reliable and extremely smart. Yet, they put up with the obvious degradation of having to share a husband. And the youngest wife- how could a man be allowed to marry someone so young? Wiz pitied Esmeralda. The girl reminded her of Ashanti in some ways- her sweet potential being soured by a beast in man's disguise.

As they walked back to the house, Wiz could not hold her curiosity any longer.

"Can I ask you a question Carla?" Now that the silence was broken, Wiz was nervous.

"Sure. I hope I know the answer." Carla was smiling a wide, knowing grin.

"Why be a second wife?"

"Why not?" Carla was baiting Wiz now.

"Isn't it hard to share a husband? I mean, it seems so humiliating. Well what I mean to say is," Wiz was aware that she was flailing.

What an idiot she must think I am.

"There is no right answer, so save yourself the agony. Some women marry for love. I suppose that's the worst reason to marry, since love is so fleeting and subjective. People fall in and out of love rather haphazardly, like a drunkard who cannot get his footing. Some women marry for children, some for money or land and some even marry for power. In my view, those reasons are more logical."

Carla stared at Wisdom for what seemed like an eternity. "Me? I married Antonio for protection. I was alone when my parents were murdered. Finances were tight. My temper kept me exposed to conflicts. So when Nazia asked, I accepted. Any smart woman would have done the same."

"Nazia asked?" Both Wiz and Thika asked together, both obviously confused about the last statement.

"Of course she did. It helps her also to have someone to share her life with. Antonio is rarely home you see. One could get lonely without companionship."

Carla knew Thika's thoughts on the subject and supported her resolve to never accept another woman into her own marriage. In Carla's eyes, every woman should be able to define what marriage is to and for herself.

Wiz continued, "Well what of the younger girl? Esmeralda?"

"That was a mistake." Carla had a frown on her face. "Nazia and I should have never agreed to that. Well, you live, learn and move on."

"What do you mean move on? Are you going to release Reli from the marriage?" Wiz asked.

"No silly. She has womenfolk here to look after her and is financially stable. Her son Pedro is here also and well cared for. Moving on simply means she will no longer be bound to Antonio."

"No longer bound to him, but still married to him? What does that mean? Does she just have to live a life without love then? That doesn't seem quite fair." Wisdom said.

"Oh but she does have love, lot's of it. From Nazia and I, from the children and from her lovers." Carla gave a little chuckle. "Antonio loves her too, in his own way. Please know that."

"Lovers?" This was very confusing to Wiz. Her idea of marriage was very different. "She has lovers?"

"Yes of course my dear. We all do." Carla flashed a satisfied grin.

Reli had a slight gap in her top front teeth and legs as frail as sticks. She covered her mouth when she smiled, and always whispered things to Nazia with her hands cupped over Nazia's ear to keep others from hearing. Reli was sweet and clean. Wiz admired Nazia and Carla however, and was confused by the life and roles they had chosen for themselves. All of the wives loved Baba Antonio Bautista in their own way. That was clear. None of them seemed to feel victimized. They would live and die for him and those children. And for each other.

"Your training is going well." Bird handed Wiz a towel over the shower door.

She emerged wrapped tight like a burrito and walked over to the sink. She shoved a toothbrush and paste into her mouth and began to brush urgently, then spit.

"Oh yeah? Then I must be close to finishing?" She was proud of herself and grinned slightly.

Her face was fresh and new. He wanted to kiss it. He stood staring at her, also grinning.

"Soon." he smiled.

Days turned into weeks into months. Bird and Wisdom, now having dissolved any awkward modesty between them before, now slept in the same bed, side by side, both under the blankets. Wisdom missed the closeness of her husband, and the now broken barrier that had once stood between her and Bird, made her feel safe and content. He had already confessed that his entire mission was to protect her, and now it showed in his actions, words and steady gazes. He cared for her and she knew it. She even sensed love from him. At first it made her uneasy, then it carried her over obstacles she knew would be impossible to overcome without it. Bird was careful not to be open with his feelings for Wisdom, and remained a silent guardian and protector of her welfare. Thika was the first to inquire about the obvious endearment they shared.

"Masai must be missing you terribly, auntie." Thika stared across the breakfast table directly into Bird's eyes. She had a slight smirk, as if wanting to tell all of his secrets, yet resisting.

"Yes, he must." The memory of her husband made Wisdom's face sadden. "I'd write him if I could. I can't wait to hold my children".

"Soon." Bird interrupted. He could hear the insinuation in Thika's tone, and knew it would hurt Wisdom.

Thika knew more than she had shared with her Aunt Wisdom. She had received word from her sister Shanzu that their father was still missing and that Masai had completed the task of marrying both their mother Wambui and Faza. He had assumed role of General and leader of the Alliance as well. Thika had softened on the idea of polygamy since her stay here with Simone and his three mothers, but thought it humorous that with all of her sarcasm and unsolicited sympathy for the women, Wisdom would have to face being in a similar circumstance when she arrived in Kenya. The growing connection between Wisdom and Bird was natural given the circumstances, but could not be allowed to mature fully.

"They are beautiful, your children are." Thika continued. "I know they'll be relieved when you return to them. When do you leave?"

Wisdom's eyes grew heavy with tears. She excused herself and went to her room. She wept uncontrollably for two hours, until Bird could stand it no longer. He entered the room and lifted her from the bed. They embraced tightly as she sobbed loudly into his chest, soaking his shirt in the process. He kissed her head, then her mouth slowly and softly, begging her to stop crying. The time had come for him to take her to Kenya. He knew it.

"Wisdom, you are a wonderful woman. An extraordinary wife and mother. Don't do this, baby." His embraced around her tightened.

"You know I can't take the tears. Please don't cry". He was whispering into her ear, his heart racing.

She looked up into his face, rivers of tears streaming down her face and nose. She was trying to be strong and dry up everything as requested, but her face betrayed her. Her face held the question her voice couldn't say.

"You've trained well, Wiz. We leave for Kenya next week." Bird was relieved to finally give her some good news.

The light returned to her face. She leaped into his arms, still crying but now with a huge grin of relief. Bird was not relieved. He too, knew of what awaited her in Kenya- heartbreak at the news of now being one of three wives. He wanted to keep her with him instead. To Bird, Masai's actions showed that he obviously did not love or appreciate her. Bird adored her and wanted to send for her children and take Masai's place in her heart and mind. But he knew that it was only a dream. The advancement of the PANA movement was the primary objective after all. This mission: deliver Wisdom safely to Kenya, then return to the States for further orders. He would carry out that mission. He had given his word to Sarg.

Wisdom spent the entire day writing letters to her children. Although for security she could not send them, Wiz decided it would be good for her spirit to write down her thoughts now, and give the letters to her children and husband when she arrived in Kenya. She sat out by the stables and talked to the horses between letters. She would stop occasionally to spot Bird, who was always cleverly in her shadows.

"You can come out now Bird. I know when you are following me." she said as she brushed one of Carla's horses.

"Not always," he said walking forth from one of the empty stables. "Only when I let you."

"Wanna go for a ride?" she asked joyfully.

Bird was instantly aroused.

He stepped closely to Wiz, lifted her up to the sky and kissed her chin. "I'll go wherever you want." he said seductively. *Stop. Too aggressive*, he thought. They raced to the edge of the ranch and back. Bird was surprised at how much better her riding had gotten.

"My kids love to ride," she said as she jumped off of the horse at the end of their ride.

Wisdom's clothes were dusty and her hair windswept, but Bird thought she looked lovely. A shiny film of sweat glistened around her neck, calling attention to the pulsing artery just under the skin. Her face was smooth and silky under the falling sun, as she stood in front of him smiling so wide that he could almost count her teeth.

He admitted to missing his son as well, and imagined all the things he'd do and say to his boy upon returning home. Wisdom knew he must have been hurting as well. He and his wife were in the process of ending their marriage and he was also away from his children. How selfish she had been to think she was the only one sacrificing things important to her. She took Bird's hand and led him to one of the stables. She gave him some paper, a pen and an envelope, then turned to leave.

"Take some time for yourself. Don't worry about me for a change. I'll be right here waiting." She turned and began to brush one of the horses again.

Bird wrote a letter to his wife and son. He wrote until there was no more room for words. He wrote that he'd be home soon. When all words were said, all envelopes sealed, Bird and Wisdom slowly walked hand-in-hand to the ranch house. The sun had set, dinner had been served and almost everyone had retired to bed. They ate together without the company of the others, washed the dishes and walked to the bedroom.

Wisdom slept a deep, quiet sleep for the first time since her arrival in South America. Her head atop the rhythm of Bird's bare chest echoed in her mind and in her dreams. The weight of Wisdom's head and the warmth of her bare body on his, took Bird to heights and depths he had never traveled. He wanted to make love to her desperately, but found contentment in this simple, restful slumber together- for now.

Wisdom would imprint the knowledge of Carla, Nazia, Esmeralda and Thika into her soul forever. She carried the women with her to Kenya and to her family. With them, she carried Dee, Ashanti, Bendi and all of the P ANA Shepsu women she had encountered. She felt she had just completed a rite of passage, and was eager to exercise her skills in a new country, among her family. Masai would be proud of her, she thought. Her children would merely love her as they always had. Her departure from the ranch was a tearful one; she would miss this circle of women, there was no doubt. She would miss Bird and their unusual bond to each other as well.

Chapter 16: Home Grown

Ngong Hills, Nairobi, Kenya

The hands of the clock were frozen. Masai lay in bed staring at time standing still. *It's been two am for at least ten minutes,* he thought to himself. His mind was heavy with everything that had transpired in recent weeks. His two sons and only daughter lay beside him in innocent, tranquil existence, and he felt like he was back home in the States; all of them haven fallen asleep while waiting for Wisdom to return from delivering someone's baby.

He wished he was back home. He wished he was with Wisdom. He wished that Karanga had not left him such an unfair task to complete. Instead, he was in Kenya. General to an army, husband to two strange women, but still as before, waiting for his beloved to return. He sighed as he looked over at the clock once again. One minute after two.

Every night before bed he had read aloud to his children until they fell asleep. He would then drift off himself, until he had the courage to return to the bed of Wambui. He dreaded sharing a bed with her. He dreaded sharing a bed with Faza. He felt as if he was betraying Wisdom, despite the complicated circumstance, and prayed she'd understand and accept the arrangement. But, how could she? He wasn't sure he even accepted it completely himself. Wambui and Faza were beautiful, loyal women and sensing his discomfort, tried to make the transition easy. Neither demanded sexual intimacy- Wambui being older and very busy, and Faza being pregnant, but it was required that he share a bed with each during the week, for show if nothing else. He knew eventually he'd have to do more, as it was the duty of any husband. He also knew that each must have her own unspoken loyalty to Karanga and probably were relieved by his hesitance. But nonetheless, he appreciated both of their patience and discretion.

"You should dress lightly for bed. It will be very warm tonight." Wambui peered over her reading glasses at Masai standing in the bathroom doorway.

She sat on the bed reviewing Alliance documents that were scattered everywhere. This was her usual bedtime routine.

Masai was nervous at the prospect of sharing a bed less than fully clothed, but he agreed and removed his shirt. He also changed into short pants and removed his socks. He planted himself in the large chair adjacent to the bed and began to read the newspaper.

Wambui chuckled to herself as she watched his head eventually bobble up and down like an apple submerged in water.

"Lie down here," she patted the area on the bed next to her. "You are tired."

She tried to conceal the smile that seemed to want to spread over her face.

Masai sighed and came over to the bed. *Much too skinny,* she thought. *Must tell the cook to feed him more.*

"I won't bite you." Now her smile was released in its full radiance. "Not hard anyway."

He smiled back timidly and lay down, with his whole body rigid as a rifle and careful not to move for fear of invading her side of the bed.

General of the Alliance was a full-time job, and the engineering position previously offered to him was gracefully declined by Masai. His political and military advisors were very knowledgeable and wise, and counseled him in all governmental decisions. The children did not attend school due to security and safety concerns, but were provided a full-time teaching staff for home schooling inside the palace walls.

Faza took them on weekly field trips to the outside, under the close surveillance of PANA soldiers. Parks, museums, concerts, movies; all frequented by the group of eager explorers when not consumed by academics. Masai was given daily updates through PANA intelligence, regarding the whereabouts of Wisdom, and the projected date of her arrival. He wondered if she already knew everything; his role in the Alliance and his marriage to two others. He also wondered what Wiz's full role was in PANA.

The news of Wiz's disappearance was disturbing to Masai, but not as shocking as the news of her involvement in the PANA proceedings without his knowledge. A wave of distrust came over him for the first time in their twelve-year marriage. Were she and his brother Karanga working together? She had kept him in the dark and took for granted that he'd approve. He did not approve. The children had been without their mother for six months already, and Wisdom had only managed to send a few letters to them all.

He was informed of her training in South America, that she had been accompanied by PANA security forces during her travels, and that she had accepted a position as Shepsu surrogate with the party, without consulting with him. Now that he had assumed responsibility as his brother's replacement, Masai was now Shepsu and Wisdom

would have to step down from her position. He was
hurt and disappointed by her selfish actions, but
couldn't help but worry about her safety. The
offensive attack on the enemy was now in full force,
and the Alliance was gaining more ground every
day. The political atmosphere was hotter than ever,
and it would be difficult for PANA soldiers to get
Wisdom to Kenya safely. If a safe passage was not
guaranteed, security forces had orders to hold her in
an alternate location until travel was feasible. All
knew that the General expected Wisdom's safe
return at all costs.

     The birth of Faza's son was a welcome light
in the dim theatre of death and destruction that was
the current war. The children were eager to help her
with the new baby, and he soon joined the ranks of
the youth wing of the revolution with them all.
Faza's love for Karanga slowly transferred over to
his brother, the new head of the family, and in her
young mind, a perfect example of integrity. She
admired his reserve in his dealings with her and she
assumed, Wambui. Faza thought that most men
would see having multiple wives and the new title
of leader of the Alliance as an opportunity to
unleash their egos and impulses onto the less
powerful. Masai however, was always respectful
and never demanding. He had stayed with her in
her room for most of her labor, playing soft music
for her, massaging her back and feet. This behavior
from a man was unheard of in Kenya, and she knew

that it was a direct influence of his stay in the United States. Faza liked it. She envied Wisdom, that she would have had such an attentive husband for each of her babies. His wonderful calming presence accompanied her through her early labor, until the midwives demanded that he leave.

"You must not be here General, it is forbidden. It would be a bad omen." The lead midwife pleaded with Masai.

He decided that the easiest thing to do would be to submit. Masai kissed Faza softly on her forehead.

"I'll be waiting right outside the door." Masai whispered to Faza and stepped out of the room.

Tradition was that after the birth, the woman would stay in separate quarters for one month alone with the baby, only visited by midwives to bring her food and attend to any health needs. But Masai would sneak into her room every night after the children were asleep, and lay with her and the new baby. He would read to them both, bring her favorite flowers, and steal away before being caught by the diligent midwives. He and Faza shared jokes, stories and a love for the new baby boy together. Faza began to look forward to the day when they could share each other's bodies as well.

Masai began to appreciate his new wives and accept them as permanent additions to his family. Faza was young, beautiful and witty. She was more open with her feelings, hopes and dreams than she had been with Karanga. She would be real and relax around Masai. She loved his children and accepted him as father to hers.

Wambui was different. She had two adult daughters, Shanzu and Thika, neither of which accepted Masai as their father. He didn't force the issue, and made sure to not be too overbearing or authoritarian with them. Thika had gone to Nicaragua initially for the summer, but stayed on later after her marriage to Bautista's son Simone. That made his dealings with Wambui easier, since it was no secret that Thika disapproved of the entire arrangement.

Wambui stayed very busy with Alliance business. Masai thought her to be very dedicated and appreciated all of her assistance. Whether she stayed busy to avoid the memory of her absent husband or to avoid the eventual intimacy with her new husband, he allowed her to drown herself in meetings, travel and household duties. She was the lone coordinator of all household runnings; menus for the chef, overseeing the curriculum for the children, supervising the gardeners, housekeepers and security team. She was a diplomat for the Alliance, and was crucial to securing new member states into the whole. When he shared a bed with Wambui, conversations were usually centered around politics, but he made sure to slip a few personal topics in. He asked her about Thika in Nicaragua and her progress as a new wife.

"Impossible, that girl!" Wambui would say with a sour expression.

"She wants to wait to have children she says. Wait until her time in the military is over. Imagine that!" Wambui's tone suggested that Thika's plans were ridiculous.

Wambui's eyes were as big as the full moon. She could not understand Masai's apparent amusement. He lay across the bed, and she was tortured by his unending laughter.

"She has plenty of time, Mum. Don't get so worked up about it." He was now wiping tears from his eyes and his middle ached.

"I am aging quickly. I would like to enjoy some grandchildren before my other foot drags into the grave!" Wambui was now starting to chuckle as well.

Masai held her face between his two hands. "No graves yet, mum. Not until I am done with you." He softly kissed her nose.

He inquired about Shanzu's studies and her plans for marriage. He even volunteered to help her match make with Shanzu- a proposal that made Wambui laugh. He had not seen her laugh since their wedding day and it made him feel good. Wambui felt good as well, something she had not felt in several months.

Wambui had mixed feelings about Masai in the beginning. She missed Karanga to the point of being ill. She had loved and cared for Karanga for over twenty years, and did not know how to share her life with someone else. She also doubted Masai's ability as a leader. But he had slowly proven himself to her over the past few months. He had made political and military decisions that both pleased and surprised her. She thought he was a good tactician and strategist, both unexpected in her eyes. She saw how very in love and in tuned he was with his children, despite how busy he got with Alliance and PANA business. She appreciated the importance he placed on family, and how he didn't seem to allow that dedication to distract him from his duties in government. He was gaining the respect of the Alliance members, and even better, the respect of the enemy.

Wambui did worry about how Wisdom's return would affect him, though. He was troubled by her absence and inability to guarantee her safety. He loved her, it was plain. And Wambui hoped that

Wisdom would appreciate the very difficult position that Masai was in, and be supportive and understanding. Eventually, Wambui would open up to Masai as well and began to look forward to the nights he would share her bed.

On nights they were to be together, Wambui waited for Masai to come to bed prior to retiring off to sleep. Whether he was working or reading to the children, she came to look forward to her husband's slender body spooned behind hers, the warmth and rhythm of his voice carrying her throughout the night. If Wisdom was to truly take her place as an African woman and wife, she would have to succumb to the African way and share Masai. There would be no other way. Wambui soon learned that she could rely on Masai to lead the people and the family, and would follow him wherever he instructed her to go.

Chapter 17: Harvest

Arusha, Tanzania

Bird nudged Wisdom out of her deep sleep. They had been flying for 14 hours and were now making their descent into Tanzania. Africa was vast and inviting, and Wisdom felt closer to her children and husband with every passing cloud. They were greeted by PANA soldiers and taken by helicopter to a base just outside of the border. Wisdom was confused by the shameless gazes of the security officers. She felt like some honored royalty returning from a glamorous trip of indulgence. She was dirty, and probably smelled like the several days of travel she had endured without the luxury of bathing. Not an object deserving of anyone's affection, surely. She tried to ignore them, and clutched Bird's arm for reassurance.

The base was busy with bustling soldiers, tanks, jeeps and armed officers. Wisdom saw no women or children, and felt a bit out of place. She and Bird were given sleeping quarters- separate sleeping quarters at first- until Bird insisted on sharing a space with her. The men were dirty, unshaven and unkempt. The days were filled with the sound of aircraft taking off and landing, remote explosions and gunfire. Wisdom was not pleased to learn that their stay would not be a short one.

"What is this, a pit stop? How long will we be held up here?" Wiz's questioning was light at first.

"I'm not sure. We are here until it is safe to travel further. I'll let you know as soon I get word." Bird knew Wiz would not accept that as an answer.

"What do you mean you don't know how long? And you consider this place *safe*?" Wiz's pitch was climbing higher and higher.

"Safer than traveling further, for now at least." Bird hoped she would be reasonable and not start to cry. "Besides, they have a medical MASH unit here. You could even work to pass the time." Bird tried to reassure her.

"I have never been some place this depressing and repulsive at any time in my entire life." Wiz sounded defeated. "There was no life here, only destruction. No plants or gardens, only dirt and metal. No laughter, no children." Her voice trailed off in a cloud of despair.

After her initial disgust, Wiz decided to keep herself busy helping in the medical quarters after-all. She was not used to caring for men with these types of injuries. Her craft had been women's health and delivering babies. That was hard to do there, since neither existed within the confines of the base. The men she had cared for in her basement clinic had gunshot or stab wounds, usually fresh. Here, men had explosive injuries, brain trauma, limbs severed and were expected to be patched up and sent back into combat.

Wiz helped with triage of injured soldiers and eventually assisted on seemingly hopeless surgeries. The limbless men and walking dead were a challenge to Wisdom's spirit. The smell of rotting bodies and hopelessness was engulfing. She wanted to help, but wanted more of an emotional outlet. Bird was her only source of light and inspiration, and even he had been dimmed by the depressed conditions.

Her thoughts moved back and forth from the desire to heal others to the desire to heal herself by escaping.

"I need a break."

She climbed onto the bunk bed where Bird was cleaning his gun. He seemed to ignore her and didn't speak. She took the firearm out of his hands and threw it on the floor.

"I need for us to leave!" she shouted.

"Not yet." He jumped down to retrieve the injured weapon. "Take a nap and try to relax."

He removed her shoes, then her socks. He cleaned her feet with a warm, wet towel, then rubbed them with his strong hands. The tension eventually left her entire body. She watched him kiss the bottom of her feet, then both legs up to her knees. Then she watched him wash her socks in the sink until her eyes became too heavy to keep open.

She wandered around the camp the second week and was nearly trampled by a herd of medical personnel running toward a helicopter full of wounded. Feeling useless and in the way, she blurted,

"Need any help?"

The sound of the chopper drowned her voice in a sea of wind and engine screams. No one seemed to hear her. She followed the mob of injured healers to the medical tent. Bird was close behind.

"Grab that stretcher there and take it to that jeep."

A man in combat fatigues was motioning to Wisdom for assistance. She raced over to carry out the command, but was stopped short by incoming fire above. Bird tackled her to the ground covering her body with his.

He grabbed her arm firmly and led her to shelter.

"We gotta get inside!"

"I can *help* them. I *want* to help them!" She looked into his eyes with desperation.

"Later!" he yelled and dragged her away.

When the chaos settled and she was in the sterile, colorless vacuum of the operating room, Wisdom stared down into the soldier's open chest and watched his heart contract, then relax. She looked across the operating table and met the gaze of Amir, the head trauma surgeon. She liked him. He worked hard and seemed sincere in his concern over the soldier's well being. Wisdom looked down again and started the tedious task of assisting Amir in removing a portion of the soldiers lung. The bullet had gone through his chest and out of his back, shredding everything in its path. After hours of blood and sweat, they closed the man's chest cavity and left the operating room feeling defeated.

"Will he live?" Wiz asked Amir on the walk back to their quarters.

"No one here is alive." Then he turned and walked away.

Several nights later, Wisdom awoke to the muffled sounds of someone crying. A woman. But where? How? She decided to go investigate, but without Bird.

"Gotta pee." she whispered as she walked over to the tent door.

There was a bucket just outside the entrance that was for late night relief and Wisdom had been instructed by Bird not to go any further without him. But the crying was calling her.

She tip-toed around the camp with her flashlight in search of the faint whimpers. When they led her to the camp perimeter, she discovered a tall tank, one she thought possibly held well water or sewage. There was a door but it was locked. She circled the cylinder tank and found a cellar entrance open. She knocked. There was no answer. She entered the cellar slowly, careful not to create unnecessary sounds. Once at the bottom, she saw someone curled up in a ball on the ground- the source of the magnetic cries.

"Are you okay?" Wiz asked. Her voice echoed around the chamber like a ghost trying to escape entrapment.

As she got closer, Wiz noticed the child was lying in a puddle of blood. She hurried over to help.

"What happened? Are you hurt?! Where are you hurt?!!" Wiz was now yelling.

The child turned toward her with a look of deep sadness. It was no child at all, but a small woman. A woman holding a listless, lifeless baby, the umbilical cord still dangling from between her legs.

"She died." the woman said coldly. "They all do."

She turned away and continued to cry over her dead child.

"Who are you honey? What are you doing out here alone?" Wisdom was concerned to the point of tears.

"My name is Megan." The woman continued to sob. " I was a volunteer health aid worker for the Peace Corp. I'm originally from Ireland. I've been living captive in East Africa for three years now."

"Captive? I don't understand." Wiz took off her shirt and handed it to Megan to wrap the child. "I am a doctor. Let me help you, please."

"I was captured trying to smuggle women and children across the border." Megan stared blankly into the darkness. Wisdom got to work clamping the umbilical cord and assessing the bleeding trickling down the woman's legs.

"Smuggling people? Why? Does your family know you are here?" Wiz asked.

"It is a war zone. Many want to flee for safety and when you are here long enough, you feel compelled to help. But my stay here was only supposed to be to help with food or shelter, you know, stuff like that. I don't know what my family knows. I have not been in contact with anyone back home." Megan's tears were drying up now.

Wisdom wanted to keep her distracted.

"Are you married? How old are you?

"I am 29 now. No, I've never been married."

After the placenta was delivered and Megan regained strength, Wisdom tried to find out more.

"Where is the baby's father?"

Surely he would have come to help if he knew, Wisdom thought.

Megan stared into the air blankly before finally answering.

"I belong to Amir. I've bore four children here in this camp, all of them his. None have survived."

*Belong? To Amir? How could you 'belong'
to anyone?*

"What do you mean, 'belong'?" Wisdom
was clearly disturbed by the announcement.

"Four of us were captured by Alliance forces
and charged with kidnapping. They frown upon
trying to take women and children out of the
country. Actually, it is a crime. Like kidnapping.
We thought we were helping." Megan turned away
from Wisdom.

"One woman has since died in childbirth,
the other two were separated from me sixteen
months ago after we tried to escape." Megan had
no emotion in her voice.

"At first we were community property.
Sometimes several men at a time. Then as time
passed, the senior officers began to claim us for
themselves as personal property. I belong to Amir."

When Megan turned to face Wisdom, all life
had left her face.

Wiz could feel the taste of bile gurgle up her
throat. The bitterness was almost unbearable.

"And what of the other women?" Wisdom
whispered after a long silence.

"Margaret belongs to the Captain and Molly belongs to the General. All of their children have also either died or been given away after birth."

Megan stood up. She walked outside, found a clearing about 100 yards out, and began to dig into the earth with her bare hands. Wisdom followed her, knelt down and began to dig also. Streams of hot tears overflowed from Wisdom's eyes and rushed down both sides of her face. The two women placed the tiny wrapped body into the ground and together covered it with cold dark earth. The sun was yawning and making its ascension over the horizon. Bird would awaken shortly and Wisdom knew it was time to leave.

"I will come see you again soon. Is that alright?" Wiz searched Megan's face for an answer.

Megan said nothing. She closed her eyes and sat motionless for several minutes. She then took Wisdom's hand in hers, and kissed it.

The next night Wisdom waited until Bird was asleep. She heard his breathing change from being rapid and shallow to deep, rhythmic series of breathes. She dismounted her bunk.

"Gotta pee," she said as she slipped into her shoes.

When she had reached the tent door, Bird's voice startled her.

"Don't visit the camp women anymore Wisdom. It can only cause trouble." Bird lay motionless on his bunk in the dark. Wiz could not see his face.

She froze in her tracks. He had somehow known about the night before.

"How long have you known about them?" Wiz was becoming angry.

"I've always known."

More silence.

"Why didn't you tell me? We can help them!" Her eyes were widening and welling up again.

"No!" Bird roared.

He had sat straight up and his voice had lost its compassion and gentleness.

"This place has it's own rules. We will *not* interfere."

"They are people, human beings, Bird! Not property!" Wiz raged back.

"Not my business. I have orders to protect and deliver *you,* Wiz. That's it and that's all! No other distractions! These women were here before we came and will be here when we leave."

Bird had now come directly to where Wiz was standing. The lantern shone on them both in the small tent and cast large looming shadows across the walls and ceiling.

Wiz stared into Bird's eyes as they both stood facing each other, shaking with anger and frustration. The sour taste was again forming inside Wisdom's mouth and her belly ached. She felt the inevitable surge of vomit boiling in the pit of her stomach.

"Amir is a pig!" Wisdom spoke with disgust.

"Amir is merely a man." Bird defended.

Wiz stood with a look of both defiance and pain. "I trusted him. I even respected him." Her voice was now trembling with sorrow.

"Humans are imperfect. We all are. War brings out the worst in everyone, but is necessary for us to win our freedom, our liberty. We can only hope some will keep there humanity along the way."

Bird stroked the side of Wiz's face lovingly.

"I believe you will be one of those people Wiz."

Wisdom had a look of horror on her face. He turned away and started to lie down, his back facing her. The silence rang in her ears for a long time before she had the words to speak.

"Have you had any of them since we arrived?" Wiz was holding her breath.

"Don't ask things you'd really rather not know the answer to." He kept his back toward her and turned off the lantern.

After several weeks on base, the day came when Bird approached Wisdom in the medical quarters, bags packed and in tote, and announced to her that they were leaving. She took off her gloves, washed her hands and took off the bloody uniform that she had been costumed in for what seemed like an eternity. She then took her place by Bird's side. She did not show any emotion- no signs of happiness or relief. She had long since lost the ability to smile or laugh during this dark interlude in her journey. They both boarded a military jeep, and drove away into the morning frost.

The ride was bumpy and hot. The dust was thick in the air, the sun shone bright in the sky. They rode by day and camped by moonlight. There was canteen water for drinking, none for bathing. After the first two days, in addition to the blistering heat, everyone started to smell badly.

The scenery changed, transformed day to day from open ranges to thick green forests. When they arrived at a small lake and the group of soldiers decided to pitch camp, Wisdom was delighted. As the fire was being started she walked over to the body of water, all while loosing various items of clothing along the way. She eased her way in and lay atop the water floating with her eyes closed, the sun basting her bare skin. She took a deep cleansing breath.

Inhale

"Aaaaaaaaaaaaaaahhhhhhh…"

Exhale

She knew Bird would soon follow. The water was warm and inviting. The earth beneath her feet and between her toes was like silk. She waded over to where Bird was now perched on the lakeside.

They hadn't spoken the entire drive thus far. She was angry with him for his callousness back at the base regarding the enslaved women.

Had he too forced himself upon one of them?

He had been so gentle and protective of her, and now she doubted if she ever really knew him at all.

Bird knew she was angry. He decided to give her all the space she needed. He would look after her as instructed, but pulled back emotionally from the friendship they had developed. It was better this way anyway. It'll make the coming separation easier when he reunites her with her husband in Kenya.

As Wiz approached Bird, he opened a small case of soap and shampoo he had brought from the Jeep and tossed it to her in the water. She began to wash her body, then her hair. Wisdom then lay back, eyes closed and body glistening wet, with her eyes gazed on the vast sky above. Her floating body moved with the rhythm of the water. Bird stood by from the muddy banks, ever watchful and on alert. Wisdom could feel her breasts now alone on the surface of the water as the rest of her body began the slow baptism. Her body lay wrapped in the warm blanket of the lake and her bare breasts firmed as the gentle breeze tickled them.

Wisdom briefly imagined Bird in the water with her. Bird's hands were strong under her back and thighs. He kissed each breast as if they were small children, objects of unconditional affection, begging for attention. He then slowly circled his tongue around each erect nipple, ignoring his now stubborn penis which grew in length and width with every one of Wisdom's moans. He stood her up and turned to hand her a towel. She was still intoxicated by his touch.

"I'll wait here while you get dressed. Food will be ready soon."

Wiz awoke from her daydream. The towel was suspended in Bird's hand waiting for her to take it.

Bird sat and watched Wiz emerge from the water, dry herself and get dressed. After the group had finished eating, Wisdom climbed into the sleeping bag with Bird and slept.

Ngong Hills, Nairobi, Kenya

Three days later, they arrived at the palace gates. Wisdom, exhausted from the uncomfortable ride through the bush, wanted to collapse onto a soft bed more than anything. The vehicle slowly entered the guarded gate, after being granted clearance from the security team, and approached the General's palace. Bird dismounted from the jeep, approached the officer in charge and made arrangements for their arrival to be announced to the General.

The General?

Wisdom was convinced that "The General" had been slain in the States, so who were they referring to? An impostor no doubt. When was she going to be taken to her husband and children? She had no desire, nor the energy to be displayed in front of their precious general. And for what? She looked at the apologetic tone of Bird's face, as he motioned for her to exit the vehicle. She stood slowly, watching his every move, but did not exit the jeep. Something was wrong. Bird could not hide that fact; his face betrayed him. He walked over to the jeep, took her hand in his, and led her over to the palace door. There, away from the curious ears of security officers, he tried to explain.

"This is it, Wiz." Bird was solemn and sad.

"What do you mean? I don't want to stay here with *the General*. Your orders are to deliver me to by husband. Take me with you Bird. Please don't leave me here." Wiz was now spiraling into a panic.

"The General *is* your husband. I'm sorry you had to find out like this, baby. He wants to talk to you inside, without any audience. Even me."

Bird squeezed Wisdom's hand gently.

Wisdom was confused and uneasy. She did not recognize any of the men standing before her, waiting to escort her to her husband. How could Bird be so trusting of these people after months of fiercely protecting her life? She was sure that there was some mistake. Masai was as gentle as a lamb, certainly not General material. And her children, where were they? The confusion on her face exposed her feelings of betrayal and neglect, and Bird had to fight his instinct to embrace and assure her. Besides, his mission was accomplished. Wiz was safely delivered to her husband. Tears streamed down her face. She moved closer to Bird, as if to embrace him, but he moved back. He slowly shook his head from side to side, silently gesturing 'No' with his lips. He knew that all physical contact with the General's wife was forbidden, and Bird had to enforce a strict moral code now that the journey had ended.

"Will you wait here for me?" Wiz asked in a low, unsure voice.

"Yes. I'll be here until you're okay for me to go." Bird tried to put a look of calm reassurance on his face.

He watched her disappear into the palace halls, escorted by an impenetrable wall of security guards.

Wiz had looked back a dozen times, each time hoping to see Bird right behind her. He was not. Why was he abandoning her like this? She ached for him, needed him. Did he feel the same way? Her breathing sped up and she became lightheaded. Was she being foolish? She was married and certainly not in a relationship with Bird. They had never made love and both surely knew their time together was temporary. But she had grown to rely on him. She felt secure when he was with her. She loved him. She was in love with him. Now she was alone.

Wisdom walked slowly, deliberately and held her breath the entire length of the hallway. The walkway ended into a large room, with high ceilings and what seemed to be a bathing area. She found a small seat near the far wall, and sat down. The security officers excused themselves, and she was left alone in the enormous room.

"I hope you are comfortable Mama Iyana. The General will be here soon. Can I offer you anything?" The soldier stood at full attention.

"No, thank you." Wiz said, inspecting her new surroundings.

The ceilings were very high, the architecture very detailed and pristine. It reminded her of Moorish Spain, with the domed ceilings and tapestried walls. Several large windows lined the room and sunlight beamed radiant rays through the stained glass on the roof, illuminating the vast bathing pool. The reflected light flickered across her face and into her eyes like restless flames. Her trance was broken by the sound of a loud, angry voice.

"You told me you'd arrive two weeks after me and the children. You had to finish some medical business at the hospital, right?" The voice was loud and angry.

Wisdom looked around, but saw nothing. It was Masai's voice, though it clearly was not the reception she had expected or hoped for. She remained silent.

"I was surprised at the news that you had actually been involved in some covert operation with PANA. I was also shocked when I was told that you were missing, and from day to day could not be guaranteed of your safety or even if you were still alive!" He now emerged into her sight.

Masai seemed taller than before and heavier. He was obviously displeased with her. Wiz had never before sensed his displeasure as she did at that very moment. He walked toward her, hot and trembling with rage. She wanted to run and embrace him but thought it not the best idea at the time. Despite his anger, Wiz was happy and relieved to finally be back with her family. He stopped just short of reaching her, and stared into her eyes with wonder and contempt.

"Speak!" he roared with all of his being.

Wisdom was afraid. She never before had reason to be, but things were different now. He was like a different person. He would have never spoken to her like that before. She too, was a different person now.

She was shaking, but kept her head up. She spoke calmly and deliberately.

"I apologize for keeping that secret from you. I thought you wouldn't allow it, and I had given my word to my brother. I had no way of knowing how out of control things would get. I certainly didn't expect to be away from you and the children for so long." Wiz took a deep breath.

"I didn't expect to be the new General of the Alliance either. I didn't expect to have two new wives, a palace and six children. I didn't expect to be waging the largest war in the history of Africa. I didn't expect that my wife, my beloved, would betray and deceive me. I suppose that life is full of unexpected occurrences." Masai's eyes were aflame.

He was now angrily wiping trails of tears from his face. He turned his back as if to leave, but his legs would not move. He was shaking with anger and felt weak and impotent.

Wisdom slowly walked up behind him and hugged him around his stiff waist. She could feel his body melt under her touch, and she walked around to his front never letting her hands separate from his body. She kissed his chest, as the tears now made their way to his chin, and dripped down onto the top of her head.

"Baba. I am sorry Baba. Please forgive me. Please." Wiz cooed softly to her husband.

She lifted her face to his and stared into his eyes, which had now softened with the love she knew was hidden there the entire time.

"I was afraid." Masai said in a crinkled voice. "I could not help you. I couldn't protect you. I didn't know if or when I would see you again." His tears were rushing down his long face.

"Shh, I know Baba." Wiz put her finger to his lips. "I'm safe, you see? Everything is ok dear heart."

He returned her embrace and lifted her from her feet. It was as if all time stopped and there was no sound or no gravity. Her mind wandered to Bird. She resisted his memory and tried to erase him from her mind. From her heart. She was finally with her husband. She had been waiting for this moment for months. This is where she belonged. Right?

Masai carried Wiz to the bedroom that had been prepared for her arrival. The long walk to the bed ignited a fire in them both that was so irresistible, they stopped short and ended up on the floor.

Between rushed, forceful kisses Wisdom and Masai managed to clumsily undress. The Kenyan heat had melted her hair to her face, and Wiz looked like a mermaid fresh out of the ocean. Masai licked the salty sweat between her breasts, and then suckled each one like a hungry infant. Wiz groaned with excitement, stroking his now erect penis with her warm, wet palms. She cried out in delight when he pushed his male part into her middle, with such urgency that she almost wept.

"God, I have missed you Wisdom." he panted between strokes.

Wisdom started to cry. "I missed you too. I'm so sorry."

She liked his heavier build. He felt strong and powerful. Masai lifted her up off of the floor and straddling his waist, carried Wiz over to the bed. He placed her face down, and while kissing her back and neck, entered her again from behind. The pair continued for what seemed an eternity, standing against the wall, on the floor, back to the bed, to the point of exhaustion, until they each succumbed to an overwhelming fatigue which carried them off to sleep.

The next morning, Wiz was announced to the children and the family. The reunion with her children was a much more jubilant one, and each child had made her a gift to celebrate her safe arrival. She cried tears of joy the entire day, and repeatedly hugged and kissed each of them with every opportunity. They showed her their school lessons, bedrooms, classrooms, their new baby brother, every secret passage and garden in the palace and all of their pets, of which the monkey was the group favorite. She loved to be back with them, and loved the new political prowess her husband had now mastered.

She waited an entire week before inquiring about the new marriage arrangement. The children seemed so happy and well adjusted. Masai was clearly overwhelmed with his new duties both professionally and socially. Still, she vehemently disapproved of sharing her husband with any other women, and made that fact known to Masai every day.

"All traditions are not good Masai." Wisdom protested. "What will be next, circumcising our daughter?" Masai resented her exaggerated argument.

"I agree, all are not. But this one is different. It is not so much good, but necessary. My role as Alliance leader means I need the respect of all of my countrymen. The respect of neighboring tribes and peoples. If I abandon my dead brother's family, I will be finished. No one will respect or follow me. PANA has made it clear that I am the one best positioned to lead the Alliance forces."

Masai paused to give Wiz time to respond. When she didn't, he continued.

"I understand your reservations baby. I had the same reservations when I arrived. You are my beloved and always will be. Please try to see the difficult position I am in."

He had cleverly kept her in a separate wing of the palace, so as not to intermingle with either Wambui or Faza. Faza did not take the children on their regular outings during Wisdom's initial return, and spent all of her time with her handsome toddler.

"Look Wisdom, I promise not to have any physical relations with the other two wives until you have given your approval. I know you are having a hard time with this whole thing." Masai promised Wiz. "But keep in mind however, that too long a delay could weaken the family and eventually the Alliance." He kissed her on her forehead. Wiz sat in silent contemplation.

Wisdom deferred working in the hospital for several months to take advantage of catching up on lost time with her children. Masai did not complain, but knew that Wisdom needed to be busy to keep from focusing so hard on the new familial arrangement. He arranged for the head of the government Health Department to offer her a position as Director of the Women and Children's hospital, a post she was sure to accept. When she did, Masai assured Wiz that the hours would still allow her ample time to care for and groom her children.

Wiz reluctantly agreed to allow Faza to resume her prior duties with the children; they really loved her and their new brother. Wiz did not want her adult hang-ups to taint their purity in any way. She would encounter Wambui and Faza occasionally on the grounds, and she was polite but careful not to invite unwanted conversations.

They all had separate dining times, and separate 'family' time with Masai- a schedule that was becoming difficult for him to maintain. Masai felt trapped in a three ringed circus, with no time for himself. He longed for Wisdom to get to some middle-ground on her stance. She resented him being in rotation every night between each woman's bed, and the time she spent with him every third night seemed to her to be fleeting and unfulfilling. She never had enough time to tell him of the day's events, make passionate love to him, get his approval of her future plans, before the sun had risen and he had to restart his action packed day as the General. She wondered was he keeping his promise to her during his nights with the other two women. She'd never know whether he was or not.

The Women and Children's hospital, in Wisdom's eyes, had been neglected for many years and in desperate need of an administrative makeover. She if anyone, was certainly up to the task. Her days became busier, her nights less frustrating. Wiz was eventually becoming more and more content now; her children developing appropriately, her husband powerful, yet attentive. Her career was everything she could have hoped for. She was now ready to face a new challenge-the challenge of sharing this perfect life with the other women of the house.

She remembered Nazia and Carla, and how she admired the selflessness of their joint marriage to Bautista, and how each had managed to maintain her own distinct and unique personality. She remembered how normal and well adjusted their children were, and how happy each woman seemed to be. She remembered Simone, and what a strong and respectful man he had grown to be, the end product of a child being raised with more than one mother. Neither of the women seemed overwhelmed or unfulfilled, simply because none had to be the sole one responsible for everyone's happiness. They shared the task of raising the children, shared the task of keeping order in the house, shared the task of keeping their husband content and productive in the society. Most importantly, the women were advocates and allies for each other. Surely, she could rise to this occasion, she told herself.

In Wisdom's eyes, Masai had behaved in this situation the same way she would have expected of any honorable man in his circumstance. He rose to the task of replacing his brother, despite his initial misgivings. He had taken on the task of army general and revolutionary leader, head of a new family, and had managed to keep his new wives and all of the children happy at the same time. He attempted to keep Wisdom's feelings in mind, so had not graced the others with his beautiful body, only his mind. She was proud of him in all respects, and thought the least she could do would be to make his difficult road a less arduous one.

Wiz announced the news of her change of heart to Masai during dinner, and invited him to bring his other wives and young son to join them for the meal. He appreciated her gesture, but told her he'd rather arrange a joint meal for the morning. That way, he'd have time to prepare the others for the transition. That night he visited Wambui to share news of the new arrangement, then retired to Faza's room for the night.

Wambui was surprised when Masai entered her room. It was Faza's night and Wambui didn't be expect to see him until the next day. Still, it was a welcome surprise and she stretched a slow grin across her plump face as she peered over her glasses.

"Lost are you, Baba?" Wambui teased.

Masai smiled and approached her, slipping both arms around her waist after she had stood to greet him.

"No mama, I know exactly where I am." Masai nuzzled her neck with his nose.

The hot whisper sent tingles down Wambui's spine.

Masai kissed her deeply and slowly as if to savor every flavorful bite of her luscious mouth.

"I have news." Masai began.

Wambui guessed silently of the coming announcement.

"She has changed her mind, then?"

"Yes."

He lay across the bed and lifted her blouse. He kissed her belly, her navel and up between her breasts. Wambui panted and raised her body to meet each kiss.

"Tomorrow, mama." Masai reassured her.

He kissed her neck and left her lying on the bed, limp and motionless. A tear made it's way from the corner of her eye, down her face and onto the bed. She begged Karanga's spirit to forgive her for loving his brother and wanted so badly to make love to him.

The light was on in Faza's room. Masai opened the door and found his young wife breast feeding their son on the bed. She smiled when she saw Masai and motioned for him to come closer.

"He just fell asleep," she whispered and lovingly gazed down upon the man-child.

The sight of her breasts swollen with milk made Masai desperately want Faza. He kissed her hands and lifted the baby over to the crib. He returned to his topless wife and licked a drop of milk that lay suspended on her nipple. He then began to suck and drink, as Faza rubbed her hands through his hair.

Her body trembled as she felt the milk rush from her body, her husband's tongue massaging her breast with every pull. Her moans became louder and louder when Masai, after having wet his fingers with milk, massaged her engorged clitoris gently until she came. Faza reacted to her first orgasm with surprise and wonder. Her new husband was full of surprises! Masai completed the night by making slow, measured, deliberate love to Faza. She was tight and wet. She was delicious and had been well worth the wait.

Chapter 18: The Morning After

Ngong Hills, Nairobi, Kenya

It took some time before Masai was completely accustomed to the arrangement. He found himself exhausted both physically and emotionally, being responsible for the well being of so many. He never had the luxury of being alone. He was never in solitary thought or quiet contemplation. The world around him was now loud, consuming and irritatingly demanding and Masai longed for solitude. Wisdom saw him struggling, but resisted the urge to interfere.

He has to figure it out himself, she thought. Besides, she was having her own struggles, both internal and external.

Wisdom found her job as Director of the Women and Children's hospital both challenging and rewarding. The maternal and infant mortality rates in Kenya were discouragingly high, and malnutrition was abundant. Still, she met the challenge head on and worked tirelessly to make an impact on the health of the surrounding community.

Under Masai's leadership, the Alliance successfully merged Rwanda, Ethiopia and the Congo into it's ranks, creating the single largest African state in modern history. Fueled by enormous wealth and natural resources, the Alliance grew in military might and exerted it's influence, both militarily and diplomatically, throughout the African continent.

Wisdom and Masai saw each other less and less. The emotional toll on them both was great and was increasingly leading to more and more discord.

"I'm tired Masai. Why don't you just sleep in one of the other wives' rooms tonight." Wisdom's voice was cold and detached as she pushed her husband away from where she lay.

"Then go to sleep if you are tired. I won't disturb you, you can be sure of that." Masai said with clear malice in his voice.

I am so tired of her shit, he thought as he flopped around trying to get comfortable with his back to her. "You are not the only one who is *tired.*"

Wisdom became more animated.

"Tired of what, Masai? What could *you* possibly be tired of? Having a harem? Having men grovel at your feet?"

She was now sitting straight up in bed, her voice growing louder and louder with each word.

"You know what Wisdom, tired of *you*! I am so sick of you pouting and sulking. I have to accommodate you like I would a child!" Masai had turned to face her.

"Faza and Wambui are trying hard to make things work. Make things *easy*. But not you, never you! We have a new life now. Deal with it! Grow the fuck up!" Masai stormed out of the bedroom that he and Wisdom shared and slammed the door behind him.

Wisdom, suddenly overcome with a mixture of rage and self-pity, fumed for what seemed like an eternity before silently crying herself to sleep.

The passing weeks turned into months and soon Wisdom found herself sluggish and overcome with fatigue. Her appetite had changed and she was having trouble sleeping well. She decided that it must be the stress of her new arrangement. Maybe she was becoming depressed. She needed a change of pace, a change of scene. A trip to visit Carla and Nazia would no doubt breath new life into her. Maybe a new perspective. She made the announcement to the entire family during a group meal.

"I'm going to be traveling for a few weeks in the coming month. I will be going to Nicaragua to Antonio Bautista's ranch for a while. I've already informed the hospital and have been approved for a short leave of absence." Wiz casually continued to eat her food.

Wisdom had already informed the children the night before and had answered all of their questions ahead of time. The adults in the room, however were surprised by the announcement. Masai sat seething with anger in silence, resenting that she had made the decision without consulting with him. Wambui noticed the anger building inside Masai, and spoke first.

"That is fantastic! I am sure they will all be delighted to see you!" Wambui shot a glance at Masai. "Will the children travel with you?"

"Absolutely not!" Masai interrupted, glaring at Wisdom with rage filled eyes.

The silence was long and suffocating. Faza fidgeted nervously with her napkin. Everyone had seemingly stopped breathing.

"Well, in that case, don't fret." Wambui assured cheerfully, "The children will be in good hands with Faza. Isn't that right Faza?" Wambui was ever the diplomat.

"Yes, of course." Faza whispered, keeping her gaze fixed upon her lap.

"Faza and Wambui, please take the children off to bed now. I need to speak with Wisdom alone." Masai never took his eyes off of Wiz.

"Very well. Come along everyone." Wambui chirped. And the entire group exited the dining room.

"Since when do you make travel arrangements without my knowledge?" Masai's anger could not be contained.

"Since I have become invisible to you." Wisdom quickly responded. "You probably would not have even noticed."

"Oh don't be an infant Wisdom! This is not some high school game!" Masai retorted.

"Trust me husband, I am keenly aware of how serious things are. In fact, you may as well know now that I am pregnant." Wiz stared at Masai awaiting his reaction.

Masai waited to speak for a long time. He had trouble finding words. He looked Wiz in the eye, then down to her belly. He put his hands to his head and walked in circles thinking for a while. And then finally, he spoke.

"How? When? You barely let me *touch* you anymore?"

"With all the commotion of the Shepsu meeting and my long travels to get here, I was not taking birth control. Why would I? I was separated from my husband? But the first day I arrived here and we made love," Wiz paused and looked up at Masai, tears forming in her eyes, "I became pregnant."

The tension in Masai's body melted away, as his face softened with the knowledge of the unexpected news.

"Why didn't you tell me baby?" Masai reached over to embrace her, but Wisdom stiffened to his touch. "Why do you keep pushing me away?" Masai's eyes were filling with tears as well.

"Because I am not keeping the baby Masai." Tears had now spilled over onto Wiz's face.

"What? What are you talking about Wisdom? This is wonderful baby. Please."

"No." Wisdom wiped the tears from her face and tried to compose herself. "I feel unseen here Masai. Unseen and unloved. Unvalued." Wisdom was choking back sobs. "I will not be an invisible wife and be demoted to just having a bunch of babies for 'The General'. This is not what I thought our relationship would be when I married you." She focused on straightening her spine and sitting tall. She wanted to appear strong.

Masai looked at Wisdom with horror, and then with pity. He had hurt her so deeply and could only think of how *his* life was affected by the new arrangement.

How selfish I have been, he thought. He wanted to wave his hand and make everything alright. Make her happy again.

"Alright. Whatever you need Wiz, I will do." Masai's voice rang with defeat. He was crying as well.

"I need time and space away from here. I cannot think here. I am suffocating."

Wiz paused for a long time, trying to still her mind and heart, and then continued.

"I will get the abortion in Nicaragua and heal there with Carla and the other women. Please do not tell the children. And this is between you and I *only* Masai. I expect you will not discuss this with Wambui or Faza."

"Anything Wiz. I will do anything. Please just promise me you will come back."

"Of course I am coming back. My children are here."

"Coming back to me as well?" Masai hung his head in shame.

"I don't know." Wiz's voice quivered with emotion. "I can't promise that. I have been so very unhappy Masai. I just need time to think right now."

Wisdom started to walk out of the room, and then paused at the door. Without turning to face him, she said

"Whatever happens Masai, I do wish you happiness. Please believe that. Wambui and Faza are nice women, I hope it works out with you all."

Then she walked out of the door.

Bluefields, Nicaragua

Carla was waiting at the airport when Wiz arrived. She was driving a dusty jeep and was dressed in a flowing, opened back sundress. Wiz had forgotten how stunningly beautiful Carla was. She was tall, round and voluptuous. She was soft yet sturdy and bold. Carla's eyes were hidden by mirrored sun glasses and her large braids peeked out from under a cowboy hat. Carla smiled an enormous grin when Wiz emerged from the crowd of other passengers.

"You look a mess, Mira!" Carla shouted jokingly over the bustling noise of passersby.

She grabbed Wiz in a strong embrace, before Wiz had the chance to put her bags down. Wisdom began to cry, silently at first and then in loud ugly sobs. She dropped her bags and collapsed into Carla's arms.

"I am a mess." Wiz finally found the words to say between gasps of breath.

"Come mi amor. Let's get you up and going." Carla helped Wiz to her feet. "All you need is a good dose of sister love, that's all. We'll have you stronger in no time."

Carla helped Wisdom into the jeep and threw her bags in the back seat. Arrangements for the abortion had already been made and the two women travelled to a clinic not far from the city.

"Are you sure?" Carla was holding Wiz by the shoulders and searching her eyes for reassurance.

"Yes. I am sure." Wiz straightened her back and slowly walked into the procedure room.

Carla waited in the waiting area while Wiz had her procedure and then rested in the recovery area. When the nurse announced that Wiz was ready to be taken home, Carla assisted Wiz back to the jeep. They then drove to the Bautista ranch, where Nazia, Reli and Thika were awaiting their arrival.

The group of women surrounded Wiz with hugs and kisses when she exited the jeep. The wave of emotion and love she felt was overwhelming, and her legs could barely bear her own weight. She felt faint. They all helped her to her room, which was

full of vibrant bouquets of flowers. Wiz could here
a symphony of song birds serenading just outside
the window.

"You must rest now." Nazia instructed. "I
will send you food to your room. Don't try to do
much. Let us care for you."

Nazia kissed Wiz softly on her mouth. The
tender show of affection caused a well of tears to
bubble up and over Wiz's eye lids.

When Nazia, Thika and Reli had gone, Carla
began the task of bathing Wisdom. She ran a hot
bath and added lavender oil to the steamy water.
Wiz stood in the room like a zombie, her face void
of life or knowing. Carla slowly removed Wiz's
shirt over her head. She unclasped Wiz's bra and
the garment fell lifeless to the floor. She pulled
down Wiz's pants, then her panties. Finally, Carla
removed the hair clasp that was holding Wiz's entire
mane of hair back and the curtains of locks
cascaded down Wiz's back and shoulders.

Once in the water, Wiz felt more at ease. All
of the weight of the entire mess that was her life
seemed to float to the surface of the water. She was
weightless. The tension left her face and neck, then
slowly her arms, belly and legs were enveloped in
peace. Carla used a large gourd to pour warm water
over Wiz's face and head. She gently kissed the

back of Wiz's slick neck and then began to wash her hair. Wiz felt like a helpless baby.

"Water cleanses all Wisdom. Just close your eyes and feel her strength. She will wash away all hurt and doubt."

Carla massaged Wiz's scalp and rinsed her head with water over and over until Wiz was practically asleep. Then Carla began to wash Wiz's body. First her face and neck, then her breasts. The soapy water covered Wiz's skin with cheerful bubbles that coated her skin with a silky shield. Carla washed Wiz's back, arms and legs. She took greatest care washing Wiz's belly and between her legs. It was the first time Wiz spoke since arriving from the airport.

"I feel lost Carla. I no longer know who I am or what my purpose is."

"We will help you find yourself. It will not be your old self, but a new one. You just need time to get to know her. And love." Carla held Wiz's face in her hands, and softly kissed her lips. "Come now, you need to eat to gain some strength."

As Wisdom stood in the bathtub, she looked like a scared, wet child. Carla wrapped her in a large green towel, and placed another on her head to hold up her wet hair. Wiz stood silent and still as Carla dried her body and rubbed amber oil all over her. She then dressed Wiz in warm cotton pajamas, a warm robe and fuzzy slippers. While Carla oiled Wiz's hair, there was a knock at the door.

"Nazia sent some food for her. May I enter?" Esmeralda waited on the other side of the door for an answer.

"Yes Mira, come in." Carla tied Wiz's hair up, with plans to continue later.

Reli was heavier than Wiz remembered. She was walking and talking normally now, with no sign of her prior illness. The skinny stick legs of her childhood were now replaced with the shapely, toned legs of a young woman. Her nipples sat atop two perfectly round breasts, that stood at attention thru her shirt.

Reli placed the tray of food on the corner table next to the bed. She then turned and hugged Wisdom before leaving quietly. Before she left the room, she remembered to add,

"Oh and Thika will bring her some herb tea when she is done eating."

"Thank you Reli." Carla said.

Wiz was not hungry. She picked at the food for a while, until Carla insisted she eat.

"Nazia put a lot of love into the food. It is the love that will heal you." Carla then spoon fed Wisdom the entire meal until there was none left.

Thika arrived about an hour after Reli had gone. When she entered, her swollen belly was the first to cross the doorway ahead of the rest of her. Wiz did not recall noticing that Thika was pregnant when she first arrived, and the site of her pregnancy sent Wiz into a torrent of tears. Carla motioned to Thika to come closer.

"You can put the tea over there for now." Carla was rubbing Wiz's back to console her.

Thika knelt down and kissed Wiz on the top of her head. The three women sat in a heap on the floor for a while, and hugged each other while Wiz emptied her entire store of tears onto Thika's plump round breasts.

"You are whole and complete." Carla was whispering over and over into Wiz's ear. "You are the creator of your own happiness." Eventually, Wisdom's tears ran dry.

The morning brought glowing sun beams thru the window and gushes of fresh crisp air to Wiz as she lay in the expansive bed. She felt lighter and even a bit stronger. There was a faint scent of hay and horse floating in her nose, and as her eyes slowly opened and took focus, she noticed a tall brown mare staring at her from just outside the open window.

"Well Hello there." Wiz sat up in the bed and greeted the shy animal.

The horse remained silent.

Wiz slowly emerged from the bed, careful not to startle the horse. When she arrived at the window, she slowly reached up to touch the animals' nose. The horse bowed it's head to give her better access.

"Good morning precious." Wiz purred to the gentle giant.

She stared into the mare's eyes and saw herself there. They were soulful. They were knowing.

Carla had purposefully brought her horse, Thunder to look after Wisdom. Thunder was known to have intuitive powers of healing and could silently relieve anyone's agony.

"She has discovered Thunder's magic touch huh?" Nazia asked Carla a few days later while handing her the tray of food to take to Wisdom.

"Yes, they are now inseparable." Carla was clearly pleased. "And thank you for adding treats for Thunder, I'm sure she appreciates it."

"She has more than earned her fair share of treats. When will Wiz be ready for travel back home?".

"I think a couple of weeks should do it. She is strong. She will overcome this."

Wisdom spent every moment of everyday with the horse. She talked to Thunder, sang to Thunder, fed Thunder, brushed Thunder and loved Thunder more and more each day. She dreamt of caring for Thunder at night, and awoke with thoughts of her new regal friend. And every morning, there Thunder was at the window, watching over Wiz and offering unconditional love and friendship. Just the thought of Thunder's gentle love was enough to bring Wisdom to tears.

"She knows you need love and compassion. She came to give that to you." Carla had silently walked up behind Wiz and Thunder in the meadow.

"How did she know? Was I that obvious?" Wiz gave a lazy smile.

"Yep, pretty damned obvious." Carla joined Wiz in a rare laugh.

"She's very wise. And attentive." Wiz reached up and stroked the animals large shoulder.

"Indeed she is. As are you." Carla took hold of Wiz's hand. "The lesson Thunder is here to teach is that we all can give unconditional love, compassion and attention to others. The wisdom is in learning to give what others need and letting that love also feed our own needs."

"I don't know if I can Carla." Wiz's eyes searched Carla's face, pleading for an answer.

"Then stay here until you can. Thunder is a very persistent teacher." Carla then gave Thunder a few apples and strolled off into the orchard.

Dearest Mother,

As I am sure you know, Wisdom is still here at the ranch. She is not fairing well with the marital arrangements back home in Kenya. As you well know, I too have not come to accept the tradition of sharing a husband and will never do so in my own marriage. With that in mind, I want to make a plea on her behalf, as she would have never chosen this arrangement if given a choice. I know that the success of the Alliance hinges on the appearance of Masai taking on the responsibility for his brothers' wives. However, this arrangement is tearing the relationship that he has with his first wife apart. May I suggest that the plural marriage be in appearance only? I am not presuming to know your sexual needs, but surely Faza can take a discrete lover or two and you both leave Masai to be with Wisdom when out of the public eye. Is not his happiness paramount to Alliance success as well?

*He will only be distracted and heavy hearted if his
true love continues to be unhappy.*

> *your youngest daughter, Thika*

<u>*Ngong Hills, Nairobi, Kenya*</u>

Wambui read the letter three times before
sitting down to write her daughter back. She had
known for a long time that Wisdom was not
adjusting well, and that Masai was dangerously
distracted by that fact. She knew her daughter
spoke the truth, but had now grown fond of her new
husband.

Very fond indeed, she smiled to herself.

He was sensitive and considerate, loving and
affectionate, and was the perfect remedy for her
grieving heart after Karanga died. She shuttered at
the thought of giving him up now. Could she
herself take a lover? She had no desire to do so.
Should she even consider it? Any of it?

Dearest Thika,

*I appreciate your concern regarding our
family and in particular Wisdom's mental state. I
agree that the situation is putting a strain on our
political endeavors and do not want to place in
jeopardy all that your father fought to achieve. I
will consider your request and discuss it with both
Masai and Faza. How is my grandchild coming*

along? No signs of labor yet? Give my best to
Simone and his mothers.

Warmly, Mum

<u>*Bluefields, Nicaragua*</u>

Wisdom sat firmly atop Thunder as the massive animal trotted through the meadow gallantly. When the horse slowly came to a halt, in clear trepidation of the coming rider in the distance, Wisdom thought that possibly someone was coming to inform her that Thika was in labor. She peered into the distance trying to identify the phantom rider to no avail.

As the rider approached, Wiz could make out that it was a male. Men always rode horses with a stiff, impersonal command, whereas women danced with the animal in a fluid ripple. The man was dark and tall. Simone would be by Thika's side and Antonio was not home. Then, as the rider approached, her breath hitched. It was Masai.

Oh my God, Wiz thought, *the children!*

As he got closer to her, Masai slowed his horse and jumped down. He walked over to Wisdom, still mounted atop Thunder.

"What is wrong? How are the children?" There was fear in Wiz's voice.

"They are very well. Nothing is wrong. In fact, everything is right." Masai's eyes sparkled with love for her.

Masai looked up at his wife and smiled. He stroked his hand up and down her calf.

"I came to visit you is all. I missed you." Masai looked at Wiz with questioning eyes.

"I didn't know you were coming." Wiz looked away.

Her heart ached and her breathing was painful. She was unsure how she should feel. She was clearly surprised and caught off guard. She did however missed him, too.

"How did you manage to leave with so much going on?"

"Wambui is running Alliance business in my absence."

"Oh." Wisdom was at a loss for words. Her mind was numb and she sat staring at Masai, blinking back tears.

"Look Wiz. I know things are crazy right now. I don't expect you to make any decisions right now or even come home with me. I just needed to come tell you in person that I love you more than anything. I want you to be happy and I will do *anything* to make you happy. It is important to me that you feel loved and appreciated. I'll do anything baby. Please believe me." Hot tears ran down Masai's face. His body was trembling.

Wiz was crying now also. "I believe you." She whispered.

She slid down the side of Thunder's saddle into Masai's open arms.

"I'm so sorry Wisdom. Let me prove myself again. Please." Masai kissed her wet face and tasted the salt from her fresh tears. Wiz could not speak. Her muffled sobs into Masai's chest was all the sound she could muster.

Ngong Hills, Nairobi, Kenya

The public face of the Masai clan continued to evolve as more and more children were added to the roster over time. Wisdom went on to have four more children and Faza, six. Wambui continued to be top military aide and was always surrounded by top security forces as she travelled, often without the accompaniment of her loving, protective husband.

They all shared every aspect of their lives together, and each woman had a distinct and infinite love for Masai. Shanzu eventually married and produced three daughters, each as graceful and logical as their mother. She secured a job as English

Professor at a the University of Nairobi and wrote several books on women's roles in society and politics.

Thika bore two sons for Simone, and lived on the ranch in Nicaragua with the other women. She joined the ranks of PANA as an apprentice weapons specialist, under the direct training of Baba Bautista. There was a relatively calm period for a few years, and all Shepsu returned to their respective duties as organizers of the people and educators of the complacent. The Alliance eventually grew to include every country on the African continent, two countries in the Middle East, and five in South America.

Wisdom thought of Bird often. She imagined being the mother of his children. She imagined giving him all the love and support he needed and deserved. She had grown to love Bird, and hoped he would live a happy, fulfilling life. Bird was also in love with Wisdom. But he reunited with his wife, and together they produced two more children, one son and one daughter. He named one of his daughters in Wiz's honor and remained a dedicated husband and father, and continued to serve in the PANA military. He wondered if Wisdom was happy. At what PANA event would they see each other again? Would they ever meet again?

Masai and Wisdom's eldest sons went on to college in America. They travelled with Masai often to learn Alliance and PANA affairs. They brought word from the States that Ashanti, now a prestigious criminal lawyer, was interested in visiting soon. She had reclaimed her daughter Divine from Mama Pearl after six years and was now married. Wisdom smiled at the news.

Wisdom trained all of her daughters, seven total, in the art of delivering the unborn child. She maintained her position as Director of the Women and Children's hospital, and also aided Wambui in any PANA or Alliance business requested of her. She came to appreciate Wambui's experience and advice on a variety of issues, both professional and personal in nature.

Faza was the educator of all of the children, and spent all of her time as head teacher of the palace school. She was passionate and energetic, the perfect trainer of the General's precious offspring. Word from Wiz's brother Sarg in the States, was that he had also married and was proud father to four sons, each with the fire of their father. Things seemed to be approaching some kind of "normal". Even better than normal. Wisdom thanked God for the ability to labor and give birth to so many children, to so many dreams and to so many wonderful experiences and relationships. She

would also ask for to the opportunity to conceive
again.

Acknowledgements

Thank you to Tovi Scruggs, Promise Flowers and Rakia Clark in their efforts to help bring this book to life. I also thank my family for the inspiration and my husband Akil El for his constant encouragement.